NEVER ENOUGH LILACS

Janelle Diller

WORLDTREK PUBLISHING

Published by WorldTrek Publishing
Copyright © 2018 by Janelle Diller
Printed in the USA

ISBN: 978-1-936376-52-0

Cataloging-in-Publication Data available from the Library of Congress.

To mothers everywhere:
If we could choose the wars to send our children to fight,
there would never be another war.

Also By Janelle Diller

Adult Fiction:

The Virus
Never Enough Flamingos
Never Enough Sisters

Children's Fiction:

For the Love of Gold

Pack-n-Go Girls Adventures:

Mystery of the Ballerina Ghost (Austria 1)
Mystery of the Secret Room (Austria 2)
Mystery at the Christmas Market (Austria 3)
Mystery of the Thief in the Night (Mexico 1)
Mystery of the Disappearing Dolphin (Mexico 2)
Mystery of the Min Min Lights (Australia 1)

WELCOME BACK! I'M GLAD YOU'VE returned. In the last book, everything had come to a reasonably happy ending, well, except for that World War II business. But you knew that was coming, didn't you? Here's a quick reminder of what happened in the last book.

My brother Ben gets an invitation to play basketball at Kansas State University. It turns out to be a life changing opportunity, but not for the reasons it should have been. My dad puts—no, he stomps—his foot down and tells Ben he can't go. Fear of the unknown can drive a lot of bad decisions. This one included. So Ben does the most spiteful think he can think of and joins the army, which is the ultimate insult to our good Mennonite thinking. We all came to regret that decision, but I'm getting ahead of myself.

Suzanne's past and all her ghosts finally catch up with her. I'd seen her push Simon Yoder—that soul stealer—from the haymow, but I thought it would be a secret I'd carry to my grave. Unfortunately, I wasn't the only one to witness the moment. Suzanne's dad had seen it too. What neither

Suzanne nor I expect is that he would be the one to turn her into the sheriff. But I guess you can't spit in your own father's face in public and expect everyone to pretend all is well.

Dad, Brother Bender, and I go lawyer hunting and discover Sam James. The case is hopeless. With Suzanne's father as the witness, the trial will go quickly and have a single outcome. I refuse to let the power of Simon's secrets win this one, too. In my own flamingo moment, I come up with the idea of contacting all of the Yoders' previous hired girls. It turns out they're an extremely unhappy lot, but they're terrified to testify. Each one believes the shame in telling the secret is far worse than what they already live with day to day.

We're lucky, though. Katie Fast, one of the former hired girls, admits that Ethel Yoder, Simon's widow, came to visit and gave her a hundred dollars. Ethel thought she was buying something that, it turns out, wasn't for sale. The power of all those testimonies changes that small part of the world.

Sam James does the impossible in Kansas in 1941: Suzanne is convicted of murder, but her sentence is light. She only has to serve until she turns 18. It's a small miracle. Okay, I like to think I have something to do with it too.

What none of us could fix, though, is the state of the world. The Japanese bomb Pearl Harbor, Hawaii, that dot on the map with too many vowels. Sam James prepares to enter the war machine of the US Army. Before he goes, he comes back to our farm and asks me if I'll be his girl. And then he kisses me. Oh my, does my heart ever thump.

Cat Peters

"Flowers feed the soul."

HADITH MOHAMMED

CHAPTER 1

THE WAR REARRANGED OUR LIVES, moving us like chess pieces on an unfamiliar board.

We spent Christmas that year with the Gerbers, Mama's family in Harper County. Twenty-six cousins lived there in that county and they only talked, never listened. I just wanted to go home, shut the door to my room, and write a letter to Sam, whose correspondence now hosted postmarks from Indiana—the land of no sunshine, or so he wrote.

The endless noise drove me to the front parlor, where the men chewed on toothpicks and dissected what these new troubles meant for farmers in general and Mennonites in particular, and then to the kitchen where even the women could talk only about the war. These same ladies who could rarely rise above a new quilt pattern or recipe now talked about Midway and Wake Island like they were the next farm over.

Two of my older cousins had already been to Leavenworth to get their physicals. The older one could have asked for a 4-F classification—a farm deferment—since he farmed a hundred and sixty acres of the family land. He didn't though because, as Aunt Lois pointed out, even though he was a conscientious objector, a CO, he wanted to do his part. His part for the next three and a half years would turn out to be a combination of picking asparagus in Colorado to fill in the farmhand labor shortage and becoming a smoke jumper in Montana to fight forest fires in the West. I always wondered if that was the part he wanted to do.

My other cousin would have leaped at the chance to get some kind of a deferment since he was newly married and his wife was in a family way. He at least received a CO status from the draft board. Mildred, his wife, told us he'd thrown up in the parking lot when he went before the board. He knew all the men on the board but most feared his old high school history teacher, who was a bugger even when his only power was to threaten to send him off to the principal. Shortly, he would be off to Ohio to work in a hospital. Mildred would tag along and live with one of her cousins an hour away until they could figure out what else made sense.

Everyone was inconvenienced, but no one was in danger. Except Ben, maybe. Possibly. We didn't know. Mama didn't talk as much. I noticed that. The flamingo in her knew when to keep quiet, even among her sisters.

In between Christmas and New Year's Eve, Ben wrote and told us the inevitable. He was being reassigned but couldn't tell us where. He didn't even give hints about the weather, let alone the continent. I suppose this was because if Hitler, or one of his many minions who worked in the US postal system, happened to capture, steam open, and read Ben's letter, why, the whole war could be lost. Our goose would be cooked. That thinking wasn't enough for Mama, though. She stayed in her room the rest of the day the letter arrived and well into the next. It was a bad time of year because there weren't any roses or daisies or black-eyed Susans to coax her out. It was the only day I could remember in my entire life that I wished I could be in school instead of at home. I stayed away from her door so I wouldn't have to hear her sobbing.

Only Suzanne stayed put in her girls' reformatory, a prisoner of her own war. Even though the two events were totally unrelated, I always somehow blamed the Japanese for Suzanne's internment because they happened so close together. I'm sure this would have made those devious Japanese happy since their whole goal seemed to be to make us unhappy.

The Kistle boys' lives didn't get rearranged fast enough, though. They still picked Emily and me up every morning and dropped us off every night and reminded us of our cowardly heritage at every opportunity. They had a big American flag in the back window, which would have made it hard for me to drive, but since I could never recollect that they actually ever looked out the rear window, it probably didn't distract them at all. In mid January, Kenny Kistle enlisted, which seemed too little, too late to me, but certainly better than nothing. Then for the next two weeks we had to endure an even deeper spitefulness from them, as though Kenny had to make his final few days with us last for the coming years.

The Sunday after Kenny enlisted, we came home from church to some of the Kistle boys' best spelling scrawled across the side of the barn. "Yeller belles." A starburst of splattered eggs dripped around the words. Dad spotted the insult from the road before he turned into our lane. He stopped the car on the road and shook his head.

"Those miserable Kistle boys! Why can't they just go off and join the war and leave us alone!" Annoyed as I was, I was at least glad that this would get Dad and Mama's attention. Now they would understand the torture of riding with those boys day after day.

But Mama just said, "Is someone calling Cat and me yellers? We're the only belles who live here. Have we been screaming at each other lately, Cat?"

Dad kind of snickered and put the car in gear again. While Mama and I got dinner around, Dad rang Mable Higbee, the Sweethome switchboard operator, and asked her to ring the Kistle farm for him. Hope rose in me that finally we'd see some good old-fashioned Old Testament justice here. An eye for an eye and a tooth for a tooth. That sort of thing. Or at least a paint brush for a paint brush. Dad had never given anyone thunder, so I didn't know what to expect, but I was at least glad he'd help me tell those Kistle boys a thing or two. Revenge would be as sweet and rich as German chocolate cake.

"Hello? Is this Kenny?" A little pause. "Kenny, this is Ezra Peters." More pausing. I had a small song in my heart for the anxiety that boy must be feeling. "Kenny, we got ourselves a small problem over here. Somebody painted some words on our barn and threw some eggs at it. It'll take some work to get those eggs off, and I'm going to need some help painting that side of the barn again." Another pause. "Well, I was hoping you and Kermit would be willing to take a day off from school this week and help me. I'll be glad to pay you a little for your work."

I didn't drop the mashed potato bowl, thank goodness. "What?" I nearly shouted. What didn't he understand about these boys? Kindness would get him nowhere except another side of the barn to paint. As soon as he hung up the phone, I said, "I suppose you'll want me to run a dozen eggs over to the Kistles since they're probably short a few."

"That's not a bad idea, Cat. We probably should send home a few with them when they come to paint." He honest to goodness laughed. He was going to pay good money out of his own pocket to those two gangsters to come and paint over their handiwork and give them more eggs to boot. Those two boys would learn two things out of this. Ezra Peters was nothing but a dumb Kraut, and there's good money in a little vandalism. The ride to school on Monday would be unbearable. Absolutely, without question, unbearable.

And at least I was right about one thing that week. The ride to school *was* unbearable.

"Well, Kermie," Kenny crowed before I could get the door shut. "I'm looking forward to earning a little pin money before I head off to shoot me some Japs."

"They're Japanese," I said. "But you probably can't spell that either." I didn't dare look at Emily. For once the entire car, not just the front seat, thought I lived with a family of idiots.

Kenny snorted. "Looks like it don't matter that I cain't spell. I can still outfox a dumb Kraut."

"Really? You've outfoxed *him?*" A little flamingo rose in me.

"He's the one who's paying." Kenny laughed like he'd said something insightful.

"Why do you think that is, Kenny?" I don't know if I'd ever said his name, so I had his attention. "Since he knows you were the one who painted the barn and threw eggs at it, why do you think he'd offer to pay you to clean off the eggs and repaint?" As I said it, I was thinking through it for the first time myself. I'm not sure I even understood it at that moment, but I had a glimmer of something poke through. My dad was many things. A fool wasn't one of them.

Neither Kenny nor Kermit were thinkers, though, so nothing glimmered for them. They just kept right on hee-hawing and talking about how they'd have a whole barn to paint and someone else's money in their pockets before Kenny went off to do his patriotic duty.

I could feel Emily's eyes on me even though I kept mine on the dull brown land out my window. When we got to school, she finally grabbed my arm and asked the obvious. "Why did he do it? Why would he encourage those boys one whit?"

She made me tired. "Emily, if I knew, I'd tell you. Do you think it was my idea? Don't you think I tried to talk him out of it?"

"I just don't get it. You heard those boys. If anything, it only made things worse."

"I don't know. He has some idea of turning the other cheek or some such other nonsense. I just wish he'd join the twentieth century is all I can say."

All that day, whenever I passed Kenny or Kermit in the hall, I got one more gibe handed to me. From Emily I got sympathetic eye rolls. She knew what it was like to live with a father with his own ideas, so at least she didn't think I was a fool, too, only the victim of living with a fool. By dinnertime, I was hearing whispered conversations from random people in the hall. Not all of them would separate my dad's silly ideas from me; I'd have to live with that going forward. As if being a pacifist of German descent wasn't going to make this war long enough, now everyone knew I lived in a family that didn't know how to ring the sheriff.

I would have gladly stayed home sick on Tuesday, except that was the day the Kistle boys were coming to paint. Emily walked across the empty section to our farm since I was going to drive. I'd told her to get there early enough that we'd be long gone before those boys showed up. As usual, though, she was on Schmidt time, so we ended up passing them on the road. They honked and waved and yelled something—I'm sure highly offensive—as they rolled on by.

The day was miserable for me. I had visions of those two boys hacking the fences down and Dad sharpening their axes. I didn't think Dad and Mama were personally at risk, but who could tell with those boys? During study time in a couple of my classes, I started a letter to Ben, but I didn't know how to explain this to him. So I tried to write to Suzanne and Sam. I at least thought Sam wouldn't sneer, but it still looked funny on paper. I ended up just feeling jittery all day and not having any way to talk it out.

I dropped Emily off at her farm first. I hadn't been there since the day I'd crossed the fields to tell them about Suzanne's arrest, and I wasn't ready for the shabbiness. It seemed that farm just kept gathering up all the sadness of the family and falling apart some more. Poor Emily. Poor Suzanne. She wouldn't even have this to come home to in another year.

The Kistle boys were done and gone by the time I pulled in the lane. The south side of the barn looked fresh, clean, and very red. The fences were still in one piece, as were Mama and Dad. Dad had started to chore already. I found him in the barn and pulled a milking stool up beside him. I wanted to hear this firsthand, not from Mama.

"Did you convert them?"

"That wasn't my plan, Kittycat."

"Well, what was your plan?" I know my exasperation surfaced.

"Just to plant some seeds. You don't grow an oak tree overnight."

Two things. First, I didn't have time to grow an oak tree. This was Kenny's last week before going off to the army, and I wanted him contrite and humbled for at least one day so Emily and I could smile condescendingly at those boys.

Second, Dad must have inadvertently planted some weed seeds because those boys were a mess on Wednesday. They must have never had two dollars in their pockets together because all they could talk about was what they were going to buy with their money that day when they skipped school again. In between, of course, talking about what a dunce my dad was. Apparently, he never took them to task for egging and painting on the barn in the first place.

"Our daddy woulda walloped us. Not your daddy, though," Kermit cackled. "He just handed us a man's wages and said we done a good job."

"We was ready if he woulda beat us, though." Kenny leered into the back seat at Emily and me. "We brought a big ol' stick with us to talk some sense into him if we had to."

This put butterflies into my stomach. "But you didn't need to, did you? That's not his style."

"Ain't his style, nothin'," Kenny repeated flatly and snorted. "He just knew he couldn't beat up on us."

"His style," I said through slightly gritted teeth, "is to make a body think. He didn't realize this would be impossible to do with the likes of you." I decided to shut up then since it occurred to me that nothing I'd say would make them think either.

They only hooted, probably since they'd run out of clever retorts in 1938.

They truly did play hooky that day. They dropped Emily and me off a block away and made us walk so the principal wouldn't see their car. When they picked us up at the end of the day, they'd treated themselves to cigars and a bottle of something in a brown paper bag, which they kept taking a nip at. By how they had to tilt the bag and the fuzzy looks on their faces, they didn't have much farther to go before the bottle would be out the window and history.

I'd never been this close to someone who'd been drinking, and I'd certainly never been in a car with anyone who'd had so much as a sip. I was as fascinated as I was terrified. Who would have guessed it? The Kistle boys got sweet, almost gooey, when drunk. They slowed down, too. At one point they stopped the car and made us all get out to look at a dead but not-yet-stiff rabbit by the side of the road. I think Emily was worried that those boys were going to put it in a gunnysack and drop it in the back seat with us in preparation for its educational tour the next day. That certainly would have been the sober Kistle boys' thinking.

Instead, they crouched down and poked it with sticks while Emily and I stood tucked against each other and the wind.

"Think a cougar got him?"

"Nah. A cougar woulda drug him off and ate him. A truck hit him."

Who cared? That's what I wanted to know. It was dead. Dead is dead.

"Kenny." Kermit said his brother's name more reverently than I'd ever heard him say it. "This could be you."

"I could get hit by a truck?"

"No. You, going to the army like you are, you could be dead like this rabbit."

The moment overcame whatever was in that bottle in the bag. Their faces looked heavy and old.

"Pray for me, Cat," Kenny suddenly blurted.

"What?"

"Pray for me. That I don't die."

If ever there was a moment in life that told me to stay away from that demon rum, this was it. I didn't want to be a totally different person, even if it made me softer and gentler.

"Now!" Kermit demanded. He stood up.

I sighed and clasped my hands and bowed my head. "Dear God, don't let Kenny die while he's off in the army killing other people. Amen." Irony sent. And lost.

"Amen."

"Amen."

"You know you have to be careful what you pray for," I said.

"What do you mean 'be careful'?" Kenny asked. He narrowed his eyes and shifted his jaw slightly.

"Because you just might get it."

The words took a few moments to soak through all the alcohol in his brain. When they did, he lunged for me, his fist tight but his arm loose and wild. I easily dodged him. He stumbled past me, catching himself just before he fell into the car. When he turned around, his eyes looked watery.

"You sayin' you want me to die?"

"No, Kenny. I'm saying there are some things worse than death." I don't know why I said it. I'd heard that somewhere and had come to believe it.

He looked like he wanted to swing his fist at me again, but Kermit had picked up the rabbit by the ears and was putting him in the trunk. "Come on, Kenny. We gotta get supper home to Mom."

CHAPTER 2

KENNY MARCHED OFF TO WAR that Saturday, just before February whipped into the state. Without Kenny in the car, Kermit's one-man harassment packed the same punch as a one-armed pugilist. Every now and then he could rip off a good zinger, but he soon figured out that he was better off invisible. Emily and I continued to sit in the back seat while he drove, chauffeur-like, alone in the front seat, so that might have subdued him. From time to time, Emily and I did ask him some polite questions, enough to find out that Kenny'd gotten his wish and had been sent off to fight—in Kermit's words—"them slanty-eyed, yeller-skinned gangsters."

"How do you know where he's going?" Emily asked. "I thought those army boys weren't supposed to write about their locations."

"He didn't. He just wrote that he wouldn't be eating no sauerkraut for a while."

"Well, you've certainly extrapolated a lot from that hint," I said. I might as well have been talking Latin, though, since neither Kermit nor Emily knew what *extrapolate* meant. "No wonder he got that tidbit past the censors."

To tell you the truth, I was secretly glad that someone as mean and misdirected as Kenny Kistle would be fighting the Japanese. I know this sounds inconsistent with believing life is sacred and all that, but frankly, I wasn't sure what we could do to the Japanese to convince them to stop fighting, so sending boys like Kenny seemed like a good solution.

The Japanese kept nibbling at us from one side and the Germans from the other. In February, a Japanese sub fired twenty cannon shells at a California oil refinery. Even though there was little damage, the event still incensed us. On the other coast, in March alone the Germans shelled and sank thirty-five US ships within sight of the US coast.

Miss Purdy, the home economics teacher, seemed personally compelled to drive the war effort in Sweethome, Kansas. From January on, she had us rolling bandages for the Red Cross and knitting scarves, socks, and balaclava caps for our boys over there. This swirled me and the other Mennonite girls into a moral dilemma. What made us true to our peacemaking ideals? What made us part of the killing machine? We decided over dinner one day that rolling bandages was life-saving. We could help do that. Knitting scarves and socks kept people warm. It didn't matter that the people we were keeping warm were soldiers. These went on our acceptable list. We drew the line at balaclava caps since they went under helmets, which would only be worn in combat or near the war zone. We avoided knitting this shifty-looking head gear even though I had a brother and a lawyer beau named Sam who might be the ones wearing them.

However, we also decided that if we unexpectedly got trapped into knitting balaclavas, we wouldn't make a stink about it since it seemed like an arbitrary line to draw in the sand and wasn't worth risking a lower grade. Besides, those soldiers might occasionally wear one just to keep warm, like the scarves and socks. I took personal pride, though, that in my last two years of high school, I managed to avoid the balaclava duty without drawing so much as a raised eyebrow. Neither of the Unruh twins could boast the same record.

Someone in the government, probably the husband of a home economics teacher, had come up with the slogan *Use it up, Wear it out, Make it do, or Do without.* Miss Purdy knew this to be the solution to the home-front effort and had taken on the challenge of putting the saying into a magnificent cross-stitch project. Every morning she brought it in to inspire us with her progress, which was rapid. By late February, she reverently carried in the finished masterpiece, full of waving flags and bombs bursting in air. While the cross-stitch was artfully done, all of us hated to remind her that the saying itself didn't pack the wallop for us that it did for her. Thanks to the Depression, none of us knew there was another way to live other than using it up, wearing it out, making it do, but mostly doing without. I didn't know where that lady had spent the last ten years, but I knew it wasn't near a wheat field.

Miss Purdy also firmly believed in doing her own personal part for the war effort. She was one of the first to invest in liquid leg makeup when we could no longer buy nylon stockings, since twenty-three hundred pairs equaled one parachute. She praised the Lord one morning in February for Duration Leg-Do Sheer-

Looking-as-Nylon leg makeup. The four-ounce, forty-nine-cent bottle promised creamy, golden, velvety skin tones. But let me assure you, the ad misled America. Miss Purdy's streaky skin and hand-drawn seam down the back of her leg convinced me that doing without had an edge over doing with in this case.

She also told us to bring in our used lipstick tubes. Thirty tubes had enough brass for twenty bullet cartridges. This was an easy one for me. Dad was as likely to let me wear lipstick as he was to let me carry a gun.

The boys in shop had their own war effort going, run by Mr. Tully, who had been a sergeant in the Great War and who daily regaled his troops—as he referred to the shop boys—with the glories and honor of war. Robert Miller told me it didn't take long to figure out that Mr. Tully had spent most of his own personal glory and honor time safely tucked away behind the lines in France, peeling potatoes and handing out gas masks to those poor soldiers who risked facing Mr. Mustard Gas.

Mr. Tully had the boys collecting everything: kitchen fat, razor blades, empty toothpaste tubes, tin cans, and even the foil from cigarette packages and chocolate bars. So Robert Miller and the other Mennonite boys had a much greater dilemma than we girls in home economics. While our work made the boys over there warm and provided them with bandages, there was no mistaking what the boys' efforts would bring. Six hundred razor blades made a machine gun, and a pound of kitchen fat held enough glycerin for fifty bullets or six cannon shells.

I thought about that every time I dipped grease out of the pot on the stove. One bullet's worth or two? If I slopped the hogs with some of the grease, did someone die unnecessarily, or did someone live unexpectedly?

Mr. Tully preached that if every family in America used one less can a week, in a year the country would save enough tin and steel for thirty-eight cargo ships or five thousand tanks. I didn't know if I should ask Mama whether to use one more can a week as a point of righteous indignation against army tanks, or one less because we didn't know if Ben would be in one of those tanks and our cans would help save his life.

As you can imagine, I spent several years during the 1940s in a state of paradox. My conscience told me killing was wrong, but two of the lives I cared most about might be saved with that extra tin can, lipstick tube, or razor blade. Or bullet.

The only thing good out of this was that it taught me that if a straight line takes you to an unequivocal black or white truth, you probably haven't thought about it enough.

The spring of that first year, the war went very poorly for us. The radio kept crackling at us about barbaric fighting and indescribable disasters in places that were only pinheads on the map. Guam, Wake, Hong Kong, and Singapore. If we suffered losses like this in dots of places like that, who knew what it would take to finally win against Japan, which, with its tentacles reaching out through Manchuria, Burma, and the Dutch East Indies, strung out the length of my fingertips to my elbow and spread shoulder to shoulder. It seemed no better in the European theater, where Hitler had started with a thumb of a country and now controlled a larger landmass than the United States.

In an ordinary year, the whole country would have been wearing black. We'd started to hemorrhage the energy and future of our country into the war tar pit—eventually we'd send several million boys and men and lose over four hundred thousand of those, at least in body. We never knew how many minds and hearts and souls the war wounded.

Even the basics that we'd managed to hang on to during the Depression swiftly appeared on the rationing list: coffee, sugar, meat, butter, tea, gas, rubber, and paper. Before long, shoes, boots, silk, dish soap, toothpaste, and even bubblegum and chocolate joined that list. Ironically, though, after living through a decade where more than the currency was deeply depressed, the war actually energized us. It jump-started a rush of adrenaline that lasted through '45, when we sunk into another fit of the blues, even though we'd just won a war. Locally, people finally had something more to talk about than wheat prices and the weather, so in that way, the war wasn't all bad.

Kermit Kistle, especially, loved the war since he loved to hate. Up until about May, he flourished. For him, all Japs were bad. All Krauts were bad. All Wops were bad. Those were his words, not mine. It made a very convenient world for him because he didn't even need to sort through the Japanese, Germans, or Italians who had lived in this country for three generations, let alone learn how to spell the various nationalities. Knowing that Kenny wasn't in the land of sauerkraut should have made Kermit jittery with all the news, but I don't think his family even owned a radio, and he certainly wasn't the kind of boy to read the newspaper in the school library. It must never have occurred to him that his own brother could be on one of those pinheads, fighting for each square inch. I doubt Kenny wrote much either. Frankly, he just didn't seem the corresponding type. And Emily and I certainly never brought up the subject on our eternal rides to and from school. Let's face it. If a skunk sprays an enemy and you're standing within range, you get part of the blessing whether or not you were the target. Kenny kept both of us in his spray range as it was. The last thing either of us wanted was to be in captivity and bring up the subject of casualties in the Far East.

I'd taken to studying the pictures in *Time*, as well as the *Life* magazines in the school library. While other girls gave up spent lipstick tubes and ladies put on dungarees and went to work in factories, my duty on the home front was to methodically analyze the rare photos with captured, wounded, or dead soldiers for the familiar Peters nose and uneven eyebrows and Sam's round, brown eyes and sturdy jaw line. Weekly, I was relieved not to see either of them in the photos. Even though I was sure both Ben and Sam were now in Europe, I also meticulously searched the photos from the Asian theater. Since the army was a branch of the United States government, what were the odds that the system would flow perfectly, always putting German-speaking soldiers near German-speaking countries or keeping attorneys far away from the butchering in the South Pacific?

I didn't realize it, but I'd also started to look for Kenny Kistle's thin face, beak nose, and slight overbite.

Not that it made a difference. Dad, Mama, and I discovered Kenny's fate the more traditional way. We came home from church one Sunday in late April to find that the east side of our barn needed repainting.

"Yeller basterds," "Hitler lovers," and a half-dozen splattered eggs decorated the broad side of the barn facing the house.

No one made any jokes this time. Dad got only as far as Mr. Kistle on the phone. The conversation consisted mostly of "Oh, my" and "Oh, my goodness" and ended quite unsatisfactorily as far as I was concerned, since there was no *You send that nasty gangster of a son over here to repaint our barn* as part of the conversation.

I would never see justice in this lifetime.

Dad hung up the phone and tried to control the twitch in his eye. "They got a letter yesterday. Kenny was fighting in the Philippines and is missing in action."

"Bataan?" I asked.

Dad nodded.

My stomach lurched. I didn't know much about Bataan except that it had been in the news for a little while when it fell in April. Some reports said a couple thousand Americans survived, some said more. The few tangled stories that flew through the country hinted at dark, unspeakable horrors for those who survived. Probably not even a Kistle boy deserved this. Certainly, a Ben or Sam deserved it less. How many Bens and Sams marched alongside other Kennys?

Mama sat down at the kitchen table, her ankles, knees, and stomach having failed her. I got dinner on and tried to talk to her so she wouldn't disappear in her room. Just before we sat down, I dashed outside and cut a couple lilac stems for the table. I deliberately set the vase next to Mama's plate and hoped the scent would keep her breathing.

None of us talked through the whole meal. Afterwards, while I did the dishes, Mama pulled out her pie pans and started cutting shortening into a bowl of flour for piecrusts. Saturday work on a Sunday.

"You're making pies?" I asked carefully and silently sorted through Gramma's erratic behavior before we all realized her train had left and she was still standing at the station. Pie-baking on a Sunday never surfaced.

Mama nodded.

"Is company coming tonight?" I asked this carefully, too.

She shook her head and sprinkled a little water over her mixture. "Seems like we ought to do something for the Kistles."

"You mean for that boy who just painted our barn with words you won't let me use even when it's true?"

"For his mother. And his father."

"Well, he'll be eating it, too. And he doesn't deserve it."

She stopped working her dough and looked at me. "And he deserved what Kenny got?"

I didn't say anything. I couldn't say that Kenny made his own choices since so had Ben and even Sam to a certain extent.

Mama sprinkled flour on her board and dusted her rolling pin. "Let's just hope that we don't need anyone to make us a pie some Sunday afternoon." The last of her words quivered. She stopped and seemed…I don't know—disoriented? Like she didn't know she stood in her own kitchen. Tears streamed down her cheeks and her mouth curled down. She put her hand on her chest to stop it from heaving, but couldn't.

We both stood there long enough for me to wonder if I should hug her, but not so long for me to move my feet those three or four steps. Then she wiped her hands on her apron and took it off. Her floured handprint on the bib of it stayed, spread out over miniature fabric lilies and an invisible heart. She left the apron over a kitchen chair and stumbled upstairs to her bedroom. Her tears now had groans and sighs and shudderings.

I stood planted to the linoleum, torn between cleaning up Mama's mess and throwing the pie dough out and being frugal enough not to even waste flour and lard.

Finally, mechanically, I picked up the rolling pin and started to flatten circles of dough. From the center to the edge. From the center to the edge. Flop it over. From the center to the edge. I draped the dough over the pie pans and crimped the edges of two of the crusts. Mama was an artist with pie edges. I was only the daughter of an artist. The best I could say was that I didn't leave any dangerously sharp edges.

While two of the crusts baked, I opened up a jar of canned peaches and prepared filling for the other two pies. Mama would have cut a peach or a tree or even a rose design in the top crusts, but they'd only get a series of meaningless slits from me. I sealed the pies and tried once again to imitate Mama with the fluting. She'd just have to apologize later to the Kistles.

While the peach pies baked, I made a lemon filling for the one piecrust and a raisin filling for the other. I realized too late that the lemon meringue pie was a mistake since I didn't think Mama would come out of her room to do the meringue. She'd have more apologies to make. I should have made a cherry pie instead. We had jars of those in the storm cellar, too.

It was only after all the pies were cooling that it dawned on me how much sugar I'd used. It made me sick to my stomach that we'd given the Kistles a month's worth in those four pies. Thank goodness rhubarb season was over or it would have been two months.

Mama didn't come out of her room all afternoon. I wrote to Sam, Ben, and Suzanne while I waited. I told them about Kenny and hoped they wouldn't notice my hand shaking through those sentences. Finally, I went out and cut some more lilacs for Mama, stuffed them into a jar, and carried them up to her room.

"Mama?" I tapped on the door and pushed it open. She lay on her bed, eyes on the ceiling, awake but not alert. "Mama?" I set the lilacs on her bedstand and gently touched her arm. Yellow light trickled in through the mostly drawn curtains. Sun and shade tree patterns danced on the floor around the open window. The lilacs took ownership of all the other spaces. Surely the scent would revive her.

"Mama?" I said it one more time. "The pies are done. Dad wants to know if he should drive you over to the Kistles." It was a strategically offered lie since Dad was already choring. I would have to tell Dad that Mama wanted him to drive her over to the Kistles to deliver the pies. That would be true at least. Half of a lie instead of a whole lie.

Mama's eyes finally drifted from the ceiling to me, but they didn't really focus. Someone should have baked her a pie if they'd only known what this news would do to her. She shook her head slightly. She lifted her hand and pointed to the dresser. "I wrote them a card. Just take that with the pies. They'll understand."

"You want *me* to take the pies to them?" I tried not to raise my voice.

She slowly, silently breathed. My anger didn't penetrate this invisible cocoon around her. Finally she said, "Take them some lilacs, too. They might not have enough of their own to tide them over."

CHAPTER 3

A MERCIFUL GOD WOULD HAVE at least done me the courtesy of planting Kermit Kistle in a back pasture rounding up the cows while I dropped off the pies. Instead, Kermit was the one to jerk open the door and snarl, "What do *you* want?"

There I stood rethinking my theology—a peach pie in one hand, a surprisingly admirable lemon meringue pie in the other, a dusty American flag hanging by the door distracting me further.

"Well?"

He could clearly see the pies in both hands. Unusually clever retorts rose to the surface, ready to leap. Unfortunately, I was still processing God and the universe in my head, so instead, I said, "We made these pies for your family. I have a raisin pie in the car, too. We feel really awful about . . . about Kenny."

The snarl twisted a little. I wasn't sure into what. He took the pies out of my hands—no *thank you*—and I went back to the car for the third one and the lilacs. The last peach pie sat on our kitchen counter at home, where Mama had said it could stay. Mama said when we ate it the pie would help us to remember the Kistles. No one had ever said peach pie couldn't be communion bread.

I handed Kermit the last pie and the card from Mama. A collection of little Kennys and Kermits—a couple of them girls—stared at me from the kitchen. He still didn't even say *thank you*. I must have disrupted his universe, too. I know both of us would have preferred staying mortal enemies because that, somehow, didn't seem like as much effort as this was turning out to be.

If I'd been two steps faster, I could have delivered the pies, lilacs, and card and left, and might have even managed to mangle my theology around enough to stay righteous and angry at Kermit. I had my hand on the car door when his mama called to me.

"Hello, hello? Peters girl?" We'd never met. I'd never intended to meet. She didn't know my name.

I turned. "Mrs. Kistle. I'm Cat."

She stepped out of the house. The screen door banged behind her. Even though she had a dumpy, short body, and chopped, graying hair, she looked just like Mama this afternoon, except that she was walking and not flat on her back, staring at a ceiling.

I couldn't help it. I started crying. Probably for Sam, definitely for Ben, and maybe even for Kenny. I didn't know. She stumbled toward me a few steps and threw her arms around me. Her softness folded around my body, and I could feel her shudder.

She finally released me but locked her elbow around mine and walked me to the house before I could turn back to the car again. She fumbled around for words about the pies and the sympathy, none of them quite right, but I doubt she'd had much practice saying those kinds of things.

She made me sit at a kitchen table, which was propped up with a cut-off fence post instead of a fourth leg, and told one of the older-looking girl Kermits to bring me a glass of water while she made me read the letter from the War Department, Commanding General, Army Forces, Washington. I drank the water out of a jelly jar while words like "regret" and "uncertain" and "sympathy" and "sacrifice" marred the page. The lines kept wavering, so I could hardly read whole sentences. Nowhere, though, did the letter say Kenny was dead, only missing. It left the most awful kind of hope, the kind no one should have to carry in case the truth eventually crushed it.

Kermit stood in the shabby kitchen by the washtub sink, arms folded tight across his heaving chest. He chewed a toothpick and stared at me. When Mrs. Kistle finally let go of my hand and allowed me to leave, Kermit trailed me all the way to the car. I pretended he wasn't there. Silly, I know. The pretense disappeared when he grabbed the car door before I could slam it shut. I don't know what I expected from him. A punch? Swear words? I shrank back into the car seat.

His body and his voice shook slightly and he said, "Is he dead?"

The question confused me. "What do you mean, 'Is he dead?' How would *I* know?"

"You prayed he wouldn't die. Did he die?"

"You mean when we found the dead rabbit?"

Kermit nodded. "Is he alive, or did you pray somethin' else later?"

"I don't know, Kermit. Prayer's not a magic incantation. I prayed what I prayed. I didn't pray anything else. He could be alive. He could be dead."

"You mean it doesn't do any good to pray?"

Oh, God, I hoped to high heavens it worked to pray since in my heart I believed that would be the only thing to bring Ben and Sam home safely. "Yes. Yes, it does good to pray." I hoped I was telling the truth. "You just don't always get what you pray for."

And sometimes you do.

What didn't he understand about that?

CHAPTER 4

Tumultuous loss rarely brings the best out in a body, especially if the body is Kermit Kistle and he's had so little practice with being good in the first place—maybe not two weeks put together out of his whole life. That first week after the Kistles got their letter, Kermit stayed home from school, I think paralyzed by grief. It gave Emily and me the entire daily drive to practice steeling ourselves against his barbs.

Emily wanted to compile lists of comebacks under various topics: Mennonites, pacifists, third-generation German immigrants, Suzanne, our clothes, our farms' smells and her farm's state of disrepair, our parents, cats. These were car-ride lists. She had also started a more general list of random insults for passing in the hall.

I wasn't sure what I wanted to do, but I didn't think that was it. I certainly didn't want to be shuffling through papers as I walked from class to class, looking under alphabetized headings for the most appropriate dig. Maybe if I hadn't delivered the pies on Sunday or met his mother or there'd been curtains on their windows, I could feel mean. Maybe if Sam were in Dodge doing lawyerly things and Ben were doing fieldwork with Dad that day, it would have been easier. Don't get me wrong. I had a certain sense of loss in not being able to strongly dislike—Mennonites weren't supposed to hate—Kermit down to his scuffed, unpolished shoes. What made it worse was that I knew he wouldn't waken to the same realization. He'd still hate Emily and me. Completely, fully, rigorously.

While Emily chattered to herself coming and going to school, I tried to think of what I *could* say, given the venom Kermit would spew. I finally decided I wouldn't say anything at all except to ask how his mother was doing and if they'd heard anything more about Kenny.

The following week when Kermit roared into the lane, Mama swiped her hands on her apron and followed me out to the car. While I got in the back seat with Emily, Mama leaned through the passenger window of the front seat.

"How's your mama doing, Kermit?" she asked. Her own eyes still looked hollow and red.

He locked his jaw and jerked his head down slightly, never looking Mama in the eye. "Ain't good."

"Well, we've been praying for you all. You tell her I'll come by and sit with her some this week if she wants."

"Thank you, ma'am. I'll pass that on to her, I will." He still only looked at the steering wheel and scattered cats beyond the car.

Mama pulled herself out of the window and looked at me. "What're the two of you doing in the back seat? You making Kermit chauffeur you around like some quality society ladies?" She laughed a little when she said it, but I recognized the laugh because it matched the one she used when she caught me reading instead of running the clothes through the wringer on washday. "One of you ought to get in the front here."

"One of you" being me since Emily gave me a look that said, *Not in this lifetime. Never. Not if my life depended on it. Your mother is crazy.*

I sighed and climbed out of the back seat and into the front and wished that Mennonites believed in reincarnation so she would have to take her turn later.

Well, let me assure you, that arrangement put us all in the wrong spot. Emily was the one with all the comebacks and no place to use them since she needed to mutter them to me. In moving from the back to the front, I took a vow of silence. And poor Kermit now sat close enough to me that he wasn't going to drop any cow pies in my lap.

When we got to the highway, Kermit stopped at the stop sign, perhaps for the first time in his life. "If you want to get in the back seat again, it's okay." He said it in the nicest voice I'd ever heard from him—no edge, no artificial syrup. There was no way I could move and retain a shred of dignity, so I just said, "That's okay. As long as we both promise not to bite." I even smiled just a little. Emily shuffled around in the back seat and rolled her eyes loudly, but I ignored her.

Kermit didn't smile, but he did jerk his head into a small nod. "I'll be good."

Other than that, not one of us talked the whole way to school or on the way home. When we pulled in our lane that afternoon, I finally looked at him and said, "Mama was telling the truth this morning. Every prayer has your family in it. We're really sad for you."

Kermit wouldn't look at me. His wrist rested on top of the steering wheel and he jiggled his head up and down a bit. I got out, refusing to catch Emily's traitor-accusation looks. I guess her family had spent so many years packing their painful losses deep inside that they'd forgotten how raw loss could be. I realized I didn't ever want to be like that.

School ended a couple weeks later, so Emily and I were done with Kermit for the summer. The Kistles weren't our kind of people, but that didn't stop Mama from feeling that sad kind of kinship folks feel for each other when losing something is all they have in common. Even though at that point we still got plenty of irregular mail from Ben, as far as Mama was concerned, he was gone for good. Even if he came back in body, she feared for his spirit. As a talisman, she baked pies or zwieback and took them over to the Kistles from time to time. And if one arm carried food, the other always carried day lilies or roses and something out of the vegetable garden.

Mrs. Kistle latched on to Mama like she'd never had a friend before. She might not have for all I knew. When Mama invited her to women's sewing circle, Mrs. Kistle took her up on it and dragged the four youngest of her brood along. Mama told me to keep an eye on the children, but I needed more like ten eyes. Apparently, those ragamuffins had never seen the inside of a church before because all morning they ran up and down and up and down the aisles in the sanctuary upstairs, shouting and rifling through hymnbooks and playing sacrilegious betting games with the rack of religious tracts while I stood, Gulliver among the Lilliputians, saying through gritted teeth, "Stop. Please don't run. Please don't play with the hymnals. Please put the tracts back. Please don't climb on the pulpit. Please stop."

Downstairs, the ladies were all quilting and gossiping. I knew those women. They were rolling their eyes to the ceiling and then to each other every few minutes. Then they'd stiffen their backs. That basement would be stuffed with sighs all morning.

I pleaded with the other younger children to play with the Kistle children, but they refused. "Come on," I said, "they won't bite."

"They shore will," Petey Miller told me like I'd just arrived from Mars. "They's Kistles. We been going to school with 'em all our lives, so we oughta know." Petey himself couldn't have been more than a second-grader. "That boy Elmer's the worsta the lot. I was you? I wouldn't stand that close to him."

Elmer only smiled shyly at me, but he did show his teeth.

If I hadn't thought it through before, that day I figured out I preferred to minister to the heathen who lived more than a tank of gas away. I'm sure I wasn't alone in that sentiment. I don't know if she finally got tired of the thunder above or the sighs and the eye-rolling below, but after lunch Mama told me to take them outside where the heat might make them a little more lethargic. Unfortunately, it mostly just made them and me grumpy. On the ride home, I made sure there were two children between Elmer and me.

It said something sad about Mrs. Kistle's life that even though the ladies of the women's sewing circle viewed her as a thistle in a well-tended rose garden, she'd never felt so much acceptance. From that sewing circle day forward until the family drifted on to squat on a new farm, she didn't miss an opportunity to bloom in our midst, which led me to the other thing I figured out about evangelizing. If you're going to reach those on the neighboring farm, find out first if they can drive. If they don't know a clutch from a gearshift knob, they'd better not have a husband who's invisible come transporting time. Kermit could have driven her, of course, but that probably would have been even worse than having it fall pretty much to our family to haul around Mrs. Kistle and as many children as she could wedge into our sedan on Sundays, Wednesday evenings, and for whatever special occasion in between. Unfortunately, cars were as wide as buses back then. We could stuff a lot of those wild Indians into the front and back seat among and on top of us adults. I'm just glad Dad never thought to show her how roomy the trunk was.

Mrs. Kistle wasn't one for nuance. Almost from the very beginning, she never missed an opportunity to ask people to pray for her son in the armed forces who was missing in action somewhere in the South Pacific. I don't know if she honestly never caught on that nobody waved flags at Sweethome Mennonite Church or if she saw us as her own mission field. Either way, though, no matter how you thought God tended to these things, there was a lot to pray about. Throughout the summer, tiny rumor fragments about those boys who'd been on Bataan darted through regular news broadcasts. Who knew what was true and what was only feared?

Mrs. Kistle also took up Bible reading and memorizing with a vengeance. She especially loved Proverbs and the many opportunities those verses afforded her to berate her children and tell them that they were going to Hell if they didn't mind. Maybe you have to start life with a Mennonite sense of fear and guilt, because it certainly didn't look like you could just start in at age ten and produce much result. Those Kistle children had been born mean and out of control, and mean and out of control they would stay. It certainly helped me understand how Kermit and Kenny had reached such an unlovable state by high school.

I have to tell you about this dream I had over and over that summer and fall. It was after we found out about Kenny, but before we found out about Ben.

Mama stands in the garden. Everything blooms as though we're standing in front of St. Peter on Judgment Day: roses, daisies, snapdragons, gladiolas—hundreds and hundreds of glads—asters, lilacs. Even the green beans and onions boast prolific, fragrant flowers. Nothing has a season. I smell it, too. Lilacs perfume the air as determinedly as roses. Even the scent of daisies—which have no scent at all—peppers the air. Mama stands there in the middle. The flowers vine around her, circling her body and twining through her hair. She doesn't

34

wear her covering because Suzanne has told her it's pointless, a meaningless ritual that only makes Henry and Simon and maybe Ethel happy. None of them are on the road to the glory land, so she shouldn't listen to them. She knows—and so I know—that even in the middle of lots of wrong things, wisdom can spring up, like a bloom on a thistle. She stands there, telegram in hand from the War Department, Commanding General, Army Forces, Washington. Ben—although sometimes it's Sam—is lost behind enemy lines. The letter only says, "I'm uncertain. I regret. I'm sorry. His sacrifice. The beginning." Mama talks to me in German, the language she'd disregarded like an extra quilt so long ago. Latin. That's how I respond. "Quos deus vult perdere prius dementat." Those whom a god wishes to destroy, he first drives mad. Latin begets German, which begets Latin.

"Is Ben dead?" I ask her. I'm under the cottonwood making zwieback because little Elmer Kistle is always hungry, and I'm worried about what he'll do with his teeth.

"Of course, he's dead, liebling! He's in the army!" And then she starts crying. No, really, she starts wailing. And then she dies, letter in hand, flowers still sprouting. My mother dies over and over and I wake up with real tears.

I hated this dream because it persisted, returning again and again. Sometimes Sam drives past and waves. Sometimes Kenny marches past and I try to tell him to write to his mother and that I would help with the spelling and edit out the inappropriate references to chicken parts. Usually, though, Ben is dead some place colorless, where the clouds and the land touch each other and make everything gray.

I woke up hollow every time I dreamed this. I think Mama dreamed this dream, too, because she looked sunken and empty most mornings. I always told her I loved her pancakes or fried mush, but what are those things, really, when you think you've lost your child to something so dark and vast that you know he'll never really be yours again? Why did I tell her I loved how she cooked when what I really needed to say was I loved the flamingo in her that knew things it didn't even want to know. That I loved *her?*

— ═══ **CHAPTER 5** ═══ —

AT THE END OF MAY, the Allied forces decisively beat the Germans at El Alamein. Churchill told us, "This is not the end. It is not even the beginning of the end. But it is, perhaps, the end of the beginning."

From the middle of Kansas, it looked like Churchill had called it wrong. Hitler, who demanded fanatical resistance that summer, seemed to keep a half step ahead. The Germans sent wolf packs of submarines to chase down and devour our ships. They weren't afraid of our coastline, either, where they sank over a million tons of ships. People died close enough to shore that if the blast and the cold water didn't kill them, they could almost swim home.

How could there be enough lilacs in the entire country for all the melancholy mothers?

It seemed only a matter of time before the Germans would land and start taking the country over, town by town, house by house. And we wouldn't have the Arctic cold and snow to slow them down like they did in Russia. I kept going to the encyclopedia to recheck population numbers. How could so few take over so many?

The tide didn't turn in the Far East, either. I didn't know where Churchill got his optimism, unless he was just saying those things to keep American spirits up and keep us in the war.

The Japanese kept dropping bombs in the Pacific, turning the sea to flames and filling the skies with smoke mountains. Our boys floated smoke dischargers in the harbors to camouflage the ships. The soldiers lived in a smoldering haze, hiding from the planes, cringing at the drone above, firing into the heavens at the bombers who were as invisible to them as they hoped their ships were to the bombers.

Burma fell. That's how the press reported it. But Burma appeared to be thanking her Buddha gods to have finally escaped British rule, even if it meant falling into the hands of the Japanese. The British didn't take any chances. They destroyed as much equipment as they could so the Japanese couldn't use it against them. The Indian soldiers left too, wearing their shorts and funny turban hats with a fan at the top on one side. I wanted to know if they felt confused that they'd fought for the British in a third country when they wanted nothing more themselves than to be free of England's condescending thumbprint on their own nation. Our press never reported it if they did.

Ben had written faithfully until he shipped out to the mystery land. Once he left US soil, he wrote often, but we received the letters sporadically. Two one week. None for a month. One a week for three weeks, then nothing again for too many weeks. The letters didn't tell us much, which left *Time* magazine and Edward R. Murrow from CBS radio to fill the gaps in our imaginations.

Mr. Murrow had a silky baritone voice that made me fall in love with him even though neither of us intended that outcome. He had a gift of making even a dinner menu sound dramatic and purposeful and an Armageddon in the Russian snows where thousands died sound righteous and holy. Although I knew we'd never meet, I secretly started praying for his safety along with Sam's and Ben's. Now that Mrs. Kistle and her younger ones came to church as regular as clockwork, I at least could spread out the burden of praying for Kenny with the rest of the congregation.

Speaking of people to pray for, just before school started, Mama let me go visit Suzanne. If the war hadn't been on, she might have driven over to Beloit with me, but since tires were getting to be as valuable as a five-pound bag of sugar and seemed to last half as long, she gave me her egg money and put me on a bus. Her cousin Thelma Balmer, who lived over by Concordia, picked me up on the other end and carted me home for a fresh slab of cherry cobbler before she took me over to "that girls' jail" as she kept calling it.

Sinewy Thelma, whose eyebrows swooped up and mouth turned down, came from the side of the family that chattered too much and drove too slowly so by the time we got over to the girls' reform school, I'd heard twice as much family gossip as I wanted. Even though she made all the connections for me—that's the one who's married to Elda's sister-in-law, or she's one of Harold's second wife's girls—I didn't much care about any of them and would have just as soon talked about the weather and wheat prices, which were finally on the rise. Or even the war. But we skirted the war because she had her own wayward son who'd joined the Army Air Forces and every day might already be dead from being shot down over Germany. Even though we could have commiserated over the shame and agony of kin who'd gone that way, neither of us wanted to pick at that sore, so she picked at other people's sores instead.

From the very beginning, Suzanne's letters had been gray, rambling epistles, full only of her daily emptiness, so I should have been better prepared for that day. When I wrote her and said I was coming to visit, her letters didn't change. That should have told me something. No excitement, no protest. If she hadn't sent me the visiting times, I would have thought my letter had gotten lost in the mail.

The reformatory looked more like a well-kept brick boarding house, with the sturdy newness and extra flourish of a WPA project, than the jailhouse in my mind. The tall red brick wall surrounding it was the only hint that this wasn't the kind of place that rented rooms by the day or week for single men, no smokers, no drinkers. Even Thelma seemed surprised and was momentarily gossip free, although I was sure she'd leave with a fresh pocketful of stories to share with the other relatives about Rose's daughter—you know Rose. She's Abe's fourth daughter, the one who lives over by Dodge and married Dietrich Peters' boy. They got that boy that joined the army. Nevermind that Thelma had one of her own in the military. A story is a story.

Thelma had brought some quilt blocks to work on. She sat and waited for me at a picnic table under an elm just inside the wall where the breeze couldn't ruffle her fabric. Her stick body looked right at home there.

Suzanne and I met in a surprisingly cheery room, full of yellow paint and lots of clean windows. Sunlight scattered over the chairs and a dozen metal tables. Sighing girls in dull brown dresses sat at maybe half the tables, each with a visitor or two. The men all had lips pursed around cigarettes. Too many of the women were crying. A tight-faced, bosomy woman sat by the door and occasionally shushed a table that got too loud or emotional. I didn't know how to ask Suzanne about all the other girls in brown dresses.

"I'm glad you came," Suzanne said, although she didn't look happy or sad. Her skin looked pasty and lifeless, all the color faded from the year spent inside. Or maybe reality. She'd cut her hair into a short bob. She looked exotic and of the world.

Even though I'd ridden a bus at Victory Speed—thirty-five miles an hour—for over three hours and endured Thelma Balmer for another hour just to be there, I still wasn't sure if I was glad to see her, so I didn't say anything except that I was surprised the place was nice.

"So's Simon and Ethel's place." Simon was dead. She should have said Ethel's place. "A jail's a jail."

"Are you afraid?"

She shrugged and glanced around. "Not anymore."

Around us people talked and sniffled and sighed. We hadn't seen each other in nine months and within five minutes had run out of things to say. I'd told Thelma to plan on two hours since that's how long visiting hours were, but at this rate I'd be out before she got one quilt block done. I had a fleeting thought that I could simply stay inside in the entryway until visiting hours finished just so Thelma wouldn't have that story to carry in her pocket, too.

"How's Mama?"

Sad. Disconnected. Quiet. "I don't see her much. She doesn't always come to church."

"Is she in a lot of pain?"

Of course she was in a lot of pain. She had lost all but one of her daughters, and Emily would be lost one way or another someday, too. "What do you mean?"

Suzanne studied me, then looked around the room at the other brown girls. For the first time that afternoon, emotion of some kind reached her face and then just as quickly submerged. "She's having stomach problems. You haven't seen her?"

I hadn't thought about whether or not she was in church until that moment. "I don't know." I shook my head. "Emily comes to church. I see her. She didn't say your mama was sick." Cigarette smoke drifted around us and through the sunbeams. My nose and throat burned from the unfamiliar stench.

"Inez and Dess write. Betsy never does."

It seemed like a non sequitur until she added, "Anna Joy tries to come see me at least once a month. She's the only one with bus money. She said Mama can hardly walk up and down the steps some days."

"Why didn't someone say something?"

"Why didn't someone ask?"

Why didn't someone. There were layers of reasons.

An awkward silence settled at our table. Given the thousands of things that bound us together as friends, we'd somehow lost the thread in our friendship that took us past accusations and into soul-searching. It shouldn't have been that way, but we'd traveled such separate roads for the past couple of years that it shouldn't have surprised us either. I didn't know why I'd even come to visit her.

"This week I'm exactly half way through my sentence. Did you know that?"

I nodded even though it wasn't true. I hadn't realized this would mark the halfway point, but I was glad we'd changed the subject.

"They'll let me complete my classes by then. I'll be done with school."

"What will you do then?" As soon as I said it, I realized I'd taken us back into the no-man's conversation land.

But Suzanne was willing to talk about it. "Certainly not go back to Sweethome. That's for sure. Although Tillie Bender said I could live with them again. She writes some." She fanned some smoke back to a neighboring table. No one even noticed.

"That was nice of her."

"Your mama writes, too. She invited me to come back and live with your family."

This was news, but it didn't surprise me. "You should. You can be part of our family." Even though it was the right thing to say, I didn't really want her to come stay. How she would complicate our lives.

Suzanne smiled slightly and shrugged a shoulder. She knew. "I'll probably go live with Anna Joy in Wichita."

I raised my eyebrows. My eyes widened.

"How could it be worse than living with all the gossip back home?"

"Still . . ." How could I start counting the ways?

"It'll be okay. She has a real job now. She's working in a factory. Boeing. They make airplanes."

I wrinkled my nose. I couldn't help it. "In a factory? That's a man's job!" I couldn't help that either.

"She's making real good money. Over eighty cents an hour! She said she could get me a job there, too."

"You'd work in a factory? One that makes war planes?"

Suzanne leaned back in her chair and shook her head. Her hair tossed, loose and free. I wanted hair like that. "If I made that kind of money, I'd never have to depend on anyone again. I could do what I wanted. Live where I wanted." She looked at me. Her voice stayed flat, emotionless, and she said, "Is that wrong? You can understand that, can't you?"

I nodded. I did understand that. She'd already made choices I never would have made—or didn't have to make. It only made sense that those choices would drive other choices. Even if I hadn't known it up to that moment, I now realized that she'd end up some place she didn't want to be. I just hoped she would have the wisdom to know she hadn't landed there solely by fate or circumstances, because a body can change the course of a life just by making hard choices instead of easy ones.

We drifted to other topics: school friends, church people, relatives. Somewhere in there she casually mentioned something that Ben had written her.

"Ben writes?" I asked. I have to admit I was surprised.

She nodded. "Not regularly. Maybe a couple times a month."

"Really?" My heart pounded a little. "Does Sam write, too?"

"Sam?"

"Sam James. Your attorney."

She looked confused and shook her head. "Why would he write?"

I blushed, feeling a little weird that all of a sudden it would matter intensely to me if he had written her, even as a lawyer to his client. "I don't know. I think all those boys feel pretty lonely over there. A letter is a letter." Although I hoped some letters were more than that. "Isn't it terrible about Kenny Kistle?"

"Who?"

I'd written to her about Kenny, I was sure.

"Kenny Kistle. The Kistle brothers? The boys Emily and I had to ride to school with?"

"The ones who were so awful?"

I nodded. "Kenny enlisted and got sent off to the South Pacific. He's missing. They don't know if he's dead or taken prisoner. He'd been fighting on Bataan."

"Bataan?"

"The Bataan Peninsula. In the Philippines."

"We don't get much war news. No newspaper or magazines. They control the radio." She giggled a little for the first time. "It's just like home."

I laughed a little also, but I wasn't quite sure what the funny part was. "The stories coming out of that part of the world sound horrible."

"Oh." She had so little emotion. I guess being in prison didn't make her very sympathetic to others in prison. Or maybe she envied that he might be dead.

The two hours inched by. We both wanted the time to be good, but she was just too lost and sad. I finally left with Thelma, not knowing what I would say to Emily when I saw her again, not wanting to be one more story in Thelma's pocket, not finding satisfaction—only confusion—in the day.

CHAPTER 6

IT'S HARD TO LOOK LIKE you just casually dropped in on a neighbor if you've got a warm pot roast and tart apple pie in the back seat. Mama stuck to her story, though, and the Schmidts certainly weren't going to let a little incongruity get in the way of eating a good, hot meal for once. Now here's the real irony: a few short years ago, Henry would have been thrilled to farm Emily out to a Simon Yoder to cook and clean and do whatever else it was that hired girls had to do, but she couldn't find the broom or light a stove burner at her own house. In reality, though, this probably had more to do with her state of mind than her state of skills.

Marie Schmidt looked like death had already come and gone. Even though we were in her house and logically she'd be the one lying on the davenport, I didn't recognize her at first because at least half of her had disappeared, wasted away to these stomach problems that we'd just learned about. Her eyes sat in dark, sunken rings and, except for a grotesquely distended stomach, her yellowing skin sagged in all the places where her body had once been. Emily scurried around to put order to the room, tidying Marie's nest of hankies and quilts and pillows, discretely tucking the chamber pot and a bucket out of sight.

How do you make small talk with a woman who's barely hanging on to life? What do you say when she says the doctor claims she should be over the worst of it by Christmas when it doesn't look like she'll see Labor Day?

We couldn't talk about the garden because Marie hadn't put one in that year, or about canning because she hadn't done that either, or about little Moses, who would start school that year because Marie never got to see him. We couldn't even talk about my visit with Suzanne because, well, because at a time like this, we didn't want to remind Marie of how miserable her life was.

We *did* talk about school starting and the milo crop. Thankfully, you can't go south in a conversation about milo, especially with prices on the rise finally. School was almost as safe, although we did have to talk about our driving plans, which included Kermit Kistle once again. What with gas rationing, this arrangement would be even more important than it was last year.

Henry was either in a back forty or intentionally avoided coming in while our car sat in the lane, so we managed to complete the visit without having to deal with that awkwardness. He probably didn't want to have to make small talk with us anymore than we did with him. At least Mama and I'd brought goodness in our hearts and dinner; he could have only brought a wagon full of guilt since he hadn't told anyone at church that his wife had poor attendance because she was dying of stomach troubles at home on the davenport.

Of course, no one probably asked, either.

"It doesn't have to be this way, you know," Mama grumbled on the way home. "Henry has enough girls who could come home and cook and clean and take care of the mama they love if he'd just admit he was awfully wrong and say he was sorry."

I knew what she meant, but the whole thing was beginning to annoy me. Or maybe it was the empty visit with Suzanne that lingered in my mind. "Seems to me that they've got to decide whether they want to stay mad at their dad and miss being with their mama in the last days of her life, or if they're willing to set those feelings aside for a while. I don't care how awful Henry is. Eventually, they've got to stop blaming him for everything and just start living again, don't they?"

Mama looked at me out of the corner of her eye. I must have sounded huffy. Finally, she said, "Well, people make poor choices in those things all the time."

Thank goodness we had a good mum crop that year, what with all the stomach problems and missing sons. Every week, we took food and flowers to Henry, Marie, and Emily Schmidt. Less often we carried the occasional vase and comfort foods to the Kistles. Mennonites never had a theology of penance—doing good works to make up for mistakes—but we've always been big on doing good for no reason except to do good. And of course, the more time you spend doing good things, the less time you have to spend doing bad things. It's not a bad line of reasoning. Still, whether Mama knew the concept or not, she paid regular penance for not realizing Marie was that sick in the first place. She organized the women's sewing circle to bring meals in several times a week and to clean every other. They all signed up, of course, even Ethel, although she only agreed to bring a meal, not clean the outhouse. I can't begin to explain to you how this could happen, but if you're a Mennonite, you're probably not surprised.

Ironically, when the church ladies started taking turns to bring meals to the Schmidts, Mrs. Kistle gladly signed up, too. There were weeks where we took mums and pies to the Kistles, and they took soup to the Schmidts. No one brought anything to Mama, though, so there wasn't true symmetry.

It all made for strange rides to and from school. Emily still wanted to hate Kermit, and Kermit still probably wanted to hate Emily and me, but if you're returning pie pans, soup kettles, and flower vases to each other, it makes it much more complicated to say mean things to each other. Mostly we didn't talk, although Kermit said at least once a week, "Not knowing is worse than knowing." To which Emily would nod wholeheartedly.

This is the truth. Single moments of agreement are better than none at all.

That fall, the whole country permanently stayed on daylight savings time. Well, I should say the clocks and people did. Our cows and chickens paid no mind to what the government told them to do; they just kept getting up and going to bed with the sun like always. We humans, though, left every morning for school in the dark and watched the colors drift up over the horizon. It was like having our own autumn bouquet and probably did as much to soften the three of us as sharing vases and stew.

If Mama thought it odd that Sam James wrote more often than Ben, she at least had the good sense to pretend she didn't notice. I knew the army had planted Sam in England because he wrote about periodically visiting his mother's cousin Agatha and her husband Milburn. I also knew that for the time being the army was smart enough to be using Sam's brains and not his trigger finger. He said he spent his days doing legal work for the military, which probably wouldn't take him close to the front until they'd used up more boys. He wrote that it felt awkward to be in that spot and that while most of the time he was really relieved to be safe, at times he felt a little guilty that his life wasn't at risk. The strange things a body longs for.

Sam had a shy style, as though he wasn't sure exactly what those long-ago two kisses had meant. Since I wasn't sure either, I never mentioned them in my letters. If it hadn't been for the regularity of our correspondence and the frequent inside jokes, I would have had to bury the fantasy that I really was somehow Sam's girl even though he still started every letter with "My Dearest Cat" and ended with "Lovingly, Sam." My neck always tingled with those words.

At one point, he asked me if I'd started thinking about what I wanted to do after graduation. He followed that question by planting a seed. "You should think about college, Cat, or maybe even law school," he wrote. "A girl like you has a brain that should be used for more than just keeping a house tidy. Wouldn't it be grand if you'd get a law degree? We could start our own practice: James & James, Attorneys at Law."

He ended the sentence with a *Ha!* It still took courage on his part. I worried over my response, which took three times as long to write as any of my other letters. I finally settled on this: "James & James? I think we could change the world or at least our part of Kansas."

James & James. That single paragraph distracted me for weeks. Actually, come to think of it, it carried me through the rest of the war.

Still, I probably depended far too much on the occasional scrabbled word or Latin witticism. I returned them in kind and hoped the British girls didn't know Scrabble or learn Latin in school since I couldn't compete with them in any other area.

We had a long, long Indian summer that year. The mums finally froze for good in November. We would now be without flowers for three months or more until the crocus poked up. I didn't know what would happen to Mama.

Just before Thanksgiving, the Russians gathered the last of their carefully husbanded reserves and encircled Germany's 6th Army somewhere on the oilfields of Caucasus, slaughtering them where they could, taking them prisoner— tens of thousands of them—if they had no choice. Now I could begin to believe Churchill. Maybe Hitler's magic was finally waning. With all of this, my head and my heart warred. My head said that surely there had to be some other way to resolve this other than taking more lives. My nervous heart sang a little song of thanksgiving every time Walter Cronkite reported a win for the Allies. It was easy to agree with just about every conversation I ended up in.

That same week, Sam wrote. He glued several dozen heather seeds onto his letter for Mama and went on and on about how beautiful the hillsides were. The censor must have been a gardener himself because he kindly let the seeds go through. Sam included another flower of sorts in his letter. He wrote about his most recent weekend train trip into the city to see his mother's cousin.

My Dearest Cat, (I loved this salutation and sometimes read it six or seven times before I could get to the rest of the letter.)

> *Last weekend I went to visit Aunt Agatha and Uncle Milburn again. You're not going to believe what happened, Cat! The train car was packed to the gills with soldiers and a few civilians. A good-looking girl about your age got on toward the end and looked for a place to sit. A half-dozen other soldiers and I immediately stood up to offer our seats. She picked out a young major and kind of pushed him back down and said he could keep his seat. She'd just sit on his lap, and then she did. Everyone laughed, but the soldier looked pretty embarrassed. The others in his outfit started razzing him about how jealous his gal back home was going to be. The girl started teasing him too, asking him if his*

gal was pretty and what her name was. The boy said he didn't really have a gal back home. She said she'd be his gal and would he send her to America to wait out the war for him there? She said she was tired of living in a bombed-out city and being hungry. The major laughed and said sure, but she'd have to go live in Kansas, and even if she got lots to eat she might rather dodge bombs than go live some place that flat and boring.

My ears perked up. I asked him where in Kansas he was from. He said from a podunk little town named Sweethome, not far from Dodge City. I started laughing and told him I was from Dodge and knew some folks from Sweethome. Did he know the Ezra Peters family? If we hadn't been packed in so tight and that girl wasn't sitting on his lap, he would've fallen off his seat I think. He laughed and said, "That's my dad!"

Can you believe it, Cat? Out of all the millions of Americans over here, I ran into your brother!!! When we finally got to the city, I took him to meet my mother's family. We had a nice dinner and then he left to go meet up with his outfit. We all thought he was a really nice boy. He's funny and smart just like you, although you're better looking. I told him that, too. Ha! Ha!

Tell your folks that he didn't look any worse for the wear. He said to tell you that I saw for myself that he still has all ten fingers, two arms, and two legs, so your mama can quit worrying about him. He'll still be able to play basketball when he gets home. I told him they should be worried about how all the pretty girls pick him out of a crowd first.

Sam wrote more about the devastation in the city, although with all the blacked-out words, basically all I picked up was that the city had been pretty much sent to rubble. I don't know why the censor thought that was a secret since dear Edward R. Murrow and his kind had been reporting the mess for over a year. Probably he needed to overcompensate with his pen since he let the seeds go through, although, let's face it, those seeds weren't exactly a war secret either.

Mama, who was up to her elbows making bierocks, didn't care about the rest of the letter at all. She made me read the part about Ben three times before she finally wiped the flour off her hands and took the letter out to the barn to read to Dad, who was milking. All the letters in the world from Ben that said he was fine didn't equal this one from Sam who *saw* that Ben was fine. It didn't matter that Sam had written nearly three weeks earlier and Ben's ten fingers could now be nine just as easily as if Ben himself had written the letter three weeks earlier.

Mama was downright giddy at supper that night. She kept picking the letter up and reading it and remarking about how small the world was. Thank goodness Sam hadn't put any casual college or law school talk in his letter. I couldn't have that conversation yet with anyone I lived with.

"What do you think it means that he's a major?" I asked.

"I don't know? Is that something important?" Mama said. "Is that something he's elected to?" She understood the subtle politics of organizations; even the women's sewing circle had them. But she obviously didn't know the first thing about military hierarchy.

Dad kind of chuckled and shook his head. "It's a rank. They get promoted and get a new title."

"Where is 'major' in the order of things?" I asked.

Dad lifted his shoulder in an *I don't know* look. "They've got privates, and I hear the term 'buck private,' I don't know if that's a rank or a term for someone who's at the bottom. They've got captains, corporals, colonels, sergeants, lieutenants, majors, and generals. I know privates are rock bottom and generals are at the top. Majors are somewhere in the middle. But I've never figured if they're above or below lieutenants and if lieutenants are above or below sergeants."

"What does it mean that he's a major?" I asked again.

"I don't know," Dad said. A tiny, worried look darted across his face. Mama missed it though.

"It probably means that the army knows he's smart, hard working, and honest," Mama said.

Ben certainly was all that. Still, Dad and I looked at each other a little nervously. Sometimes you get promoted because of the special things you do. But neither of us wanted to spoil Mama's moment because she hadn't had many hours in the last couple years where her shoulders didn't droop slightly and her eyes didn't look a little empty. We didn't want to take these minutes away from her since we didn't know how long it would last.

A few days later, Ben's letter came. He completely left out the story about the girl on his lap—which only told me how many other stories we'd never heard—and went on to talk about the coincidence of running into this Sam James fellow that knew us all. Ben thought he was quite a likable chap and was planning to meet up with him again the weekend after Thanksgiving, which meant that the two would have already met up again before we knew they'd met the first time. This felt eerie for some reason, although it shouldn't have. Letters are always like that.

Mama positively floated. If they kept up their visits, she'd have an eyewitness to Ben's safety every few weeks. For her, this was almost as good—no, this was even better than a letter from Ben saying he was okay. As for me, I didn't mind it so much either. Ben had his own charm. It wouldn't hurt if Sam learned to like him as much as the rest of us.

CHAPTER 7

Marie Schmidt's doctor was right about one thing: she was over the worst of her troubles by Christmas. She died Christmas Eve.

In the strange way that coincidences grip a body, we all had this one to contend with. Traditionally, after the Christmas Eve program, the young folks from church always went caroling. That year, we had to weigh the value of caroling to the country folks against the gas coupons it would take and had pretty much decided to walk up and down the streets of Sweethome. In the spirit of the season, President Roosevelt should have issued an extra coupon per family, but he didn't so we had to be careful with what we had.

Someone, maybe it was even me, suggested that we still go out to the Schmidts' to sing since Marie would really appreciate it. At the end of the evening, we stuffed ourselves into the cab and bed of a pickup truck and drove on out to the Schmidt farm. The moonlight carried us, lifting empty cottonwood branches higher to the heavens and shining silvery strings of light like tinsel along the furrows in the fields. We started out singing, but something stronger than music took hold of our hearts and left us silent. The shadows flitted past us, carving darkness out of the light but seeming to carve light out of the darkness. I realized I was praying for peace on earth in those troubled times. I wondered if the others were praying, too, and if in that open truck bed, bundled together like we were—yet unshackled by rafters and pews, sermons and corporate prayers—what we were asking for wasn't finally being heard.

We pulled into the Schmidt lane, still silent. A single downstairs light burned in the front parlor. We gathered on the sagging front porch and began, first with "Hark! The Herald Angels Sing!" then "O Little Town of Bethlehem" and then "Silent Night." We sounded angelic in that midnight hour, even though no one in our group was older than twenty-two or twenty-three, and none had any formal music training. Every one of us, though, had feasted on endless a cappella four-part harmony since we were in the womb, so there was an untrained beauty that echoed in the shivery night. No more lights came on, and no one came to the door, but we sang some more anyway. The round trip would take over a gallon of gas. We were going to make it worth our while.

Finally, we began "Joy to the World," our signal that only "We Wish You a Merry Christmas" would follow, and we'd be gone.

A second light finally came on and the front door opened. I stiffened slightly, I know. Henry stood there, an arm's length away from me on the other side of the screen door. I couldn't see Emily. Henry tried to sing along, but I could tell that tears flowed down his cheeks. He took out a crumpled red bandana and wiped his face and then wiped it again. Finally, he opened the screen door and leaned over to me. I thought he said, "Marie's gone."

"What?"

He took a deep breath and leaned closer. "Marie's gone. She just passed. It means a lot that you drove all the way out here. The last thing she heard was this heavenly choir." He stepped back in the house and closed the door.

A spirited "Joy to the World" died out at the end of the second verse. The wind shivered through us as whispered voices passed the news. The starry, starry night urged us to do something: acknowledge, bring comfort, leave. Maybe not in that order, though, which only incited confusion. Finally, I started singing "Amazing Grace." It certainly wasn't a Christmas carol and wasn't exactly a funeral song, but it was the right one, at least for Henry. By the time my voice got lost in tears, the other voices carried the song, unaware of the power of the words at this moment.

$$\text{———} \equiv\!\equiv \text{CHAPTER 8} \equiv\!\equiv \text{———}$$

T HE S ATURDAY AFTER THE FUNERAL , Mama let me ride the bus to Beloit with Inez, Tim, Dess, and Moses. Emily, who felt the loss of Suzanne even more keenly than the rest of us, should have been along, too. She told me later that her dad had just snorted in disbelief that she'd even asked to go. "He told me Suzanne should rot there alone. That she doesn't deserve to have family." She snorted herself and added, "He's the one who should rot alone without family."

It took us almost four and a half hours instead of three because not only did we have to contend with the thirty-five miles per hour victory speed, but at every stop we had to wait for all the girls and mothers to say goodbye to their soldiers. The hankie manufacturers were having a boom year. I tried not to think about Sam or Ben.

It also took extra time for the driver to find a cranny to stuff all the duffel bags into the baggage boxes and squeeze yet one more green or gray or blue uniform into the seats. The Kansas Bus and Transport Company had at least warned us, though. This disclaimer hung above the driver's head: "It is only fair to tell you that buses are crowded these days. You'll be more comfortable at home." They were certainly right about that, but there wasn't much we could do about the mission we were on, so like we did about everything else, we simply endured.

We had to keep enduring even after we arrived in Concordia since Mama's cousin Thelma picked us up. Fortunately, the Schmidt sisters were born with that chatterbug nature. They kept Thelma distracted in the front seat with details about Marie's final moments and her funeral and never even let themselves get cornered into an awkward moment about Suzanne. Tim and I sat in the back seat and let Moses use our knees for—as he called it—"highaways" for his busy trucks. Even though the little boy didn't have an ounce of Tim in him, he'd somehow adopted the man's quiet nature. He had a sweet shyness to him that made you want to wrap your arms around him and tousle his blond curls. It was almost good that Marie hadn't seen Moses every Sunday or she would have been even sadder about the joy that Henry had sliced out of their lives.

Ordinarily, the jail people only let a girl have two visitors at a time, but since Moses only counted for about a quarter of a person and the circumstances were extra sad, they let all of us sit at a table with Dess in the sunny yellow room with all the windows. I kind of regretted being there at all. I don't know what I'd been thinking when I begged Mama to let me tag along. As folks had filed out of the church and into the graveyard, Dess had motioned me over to where all the family but Henry—who sat an empty chair away—huddled under the green funeral canopy, bodies tilting into the gray wind, wool flannel coats flapping parallel to the ground. Emotions must have clouded out memory because at that moment, I had sincerely wanted to see Suzanne.

We all sat at that table, our knees touching, our thoughts fragmented. Suzanne spread the Christmas Day telegram out on the table. It had been folded and unfolded, read, and read some more. Inez and Dess, who'd been surprisingly unemotional all morning, now couldn't stop sniffling and wiping their eyes and noses. Tim held Moses and worked earnestly to keep the little boy quiet. It was a ruse, though, since Moses seemed perfectly content to find new highaways on the table for his trucks and wasn't about to make more than a puttering engine noise.

Somebody had to talk even though none of us had anything to say that wouldn't make us cry even more. Finally, I said, "I saw your mama most weeks when Mama and I took food over." It was a whole lot more than anyone else at the table could say.

Suzanne nodded. Her chin rested on her hands, her elbows on the table.

"She asked about you every time I went since she knew I saw you last summer." I never said that her other daughters should have visited her every week. No, every day. I think I kept that inside my head.

Suzanne nodded again. She kept swallowing.

"I always told her that you weren't afraid to be here. That made her happy." I'm pretty sure I didn't say that Marie should have had Inez or Dess drive her over to see Suzanne.

"What will happen to Emily?"

I looked at Dess and Inez and waited until I realized they didn't know.

"The Kistles are moving to a farm over by Pratt. Emily and I are going to live in town with Edwin and Tilly Bender and walk to school."

"Why wouldn't you just drive?" Suzanne asked.

"Dad's worried that he won't have enough gas coupons for harvest." What would it be like not to have to weigh every decision based on gas coupons? What would it be like not to even know that gas was that tightly rationed? Hadn't I written to her about this?

Suzanne watched the people at the next table for a minute. They smoked and sighed, which I already knew to be the language of this place. Not a stitch of emotion surfaced. She finally looked back at Inez and Dess. "Remember how on Christmas Eve we'd go to the program at church and then come home and make caramel popcorn? It was the one night of the year that Mama went to all that trouble. And then we'd sit at the table and eat the popcorn and go around the table verse by verse and recite the Christmas story from memory?"

Inez and Dess nodded. Their tears flooded over again.

"Now we have a new Christmas Eve memory. And none of us were there for it."

It didn't have to be that way. I wanted to shout it. I was afraid I had shouted it. Instead, I think I said, "Except Emily."

"And Cat," Dess said.

Suzanne looked at me, tilting her head and furrowing her brow a tiny bit. She hadn't heard.

"We—the young folks from church—were caroling at your house when she died. Your mama took her last breath during 'Silent Night.'"

Suzanne turned to watch the people at the next table again. This time I could see she was fighting tears. When she looked back at us, she hardly talked above a whisper. "Was she in a lot of pain at the end?"

"I don't know. We weren't in the house. We didn't . . . we didn't know she was that close to the end. It was just a coincidence." I said it but I didn't believe it was that simple. I felt edgy and realized I wanted desperately to be at another table, being part of someone else's misery or, better yet, piecing quilt blocks and avoiding conversation in the car with Thelma.

"But you were there."

I nodded. The three Schmidt girls battled their own demons but kept creating more. My insides kept churning. You can't surgically remove someone from your life. They'd tried to do that with Henry, but instead of just taking out a bad spot, they'd severed an entire limb. Couldn't they see this?

"Why weren't *you* there?" I didn't mean to blurt it out.

Inez and Dess looked confused. Tim gave me an odd look. Moses just kept puttering his truck.

Dess asked the questions for all of them. "What do you mean? After what Dad did? After what he did to Suzanne? To each of us? How could we ever go home again?" She shook her head with each word, disbelieving that I would say such a thing.

I should have just shut my mouth. I should have apologized and said I knew Henry had made horrible decisions that would forever leave ugly scars on their hearts. I should have just let them believe that, even now, Henry continued to ruin their lives. "That was wrong. It was wrong then and it's still wrong. But look at what you all lost because . . ." Because what? Because they stayed angry with their dad? Because they couldn't do the impossible and forgive him? ". . . because you couldn't be there for your mama." I shouldn't have kept salting the wound.

Suzanne clenched her teeth but didn't talk.

Inez sobbed and shook her head. "You don't understand."

I didn't understand. I knew that. But they didn't either.

"We can't *ever* forgive him."

"Then it'll never be over. Even for Moses."

CHAPTER 9

I'VE ALWAYS STRUGGLED WITH A diet heavy on shoe leather, so it didn't come as any surprise to me that the bus ride back to Sweethome was pretty tense. I don't know why it was that I'd figured out I needed to keep my mouth shut around Kermit Kistle—and managed to even make some peace with him—but didn't know how to mind my own business with my one-time best friend's sisters.

We circled the topic at least three or four more times before the bus stopped in Sweethome. Each time Dess and Inez said I just didn't understand. Henry had destroyed their lives. They never wanted to see him again. I could only repeat, "Look what you lost, though."

Fortunately, even though Emily must have gotten the full jail story from her sisters in a letter, she had more of Marie than Henry in her and consequently had a hard time holding a grudge. She tried to be icy to me the first few days we moved into the Benders' house, but being the motherless child that she was, she needed a friend every bit as much as I did, so it didn't last long.

The Benders had three whole bedrooms on their second floor, giving Emily and me our own rooms. A narrow, low-ceilinged landing separated the three bedrooms. My first week I fell asleep to Edwin's rattley breathing and Emily's quiet sobbing. I wanted to cry, too, but compared to the rest of the world, I didn't have any good reason to feel teary. I still had a mother and father, a brother, a house, and a country. Even though I wanted desperately to be back in my own bed, listening to my own dad's arhythmic snores, I just gritted my teeth and wrote letters in my head to Sam, some of which found their way to paper, but the wittiest ones drifted between wakefulness and sleep and just dissipated. Frankly, I was mad at the Germans for starting the war and mad at Roosevelt for thinking our extra five commuting gallons a week would make a difference in the war effort. Some days I was even mad at the Kistles for moving and taking away my ride to school. Needless to say, I kept my mouth shut about those ideas.

The first Friday, Dad picked Emily and me up from the Benders'. The next week Henry came. After that, only Dad picked me up. Emily stayed at the Benders or waited patiently for Tim and Moses to come get her for the weekend. It was only one more battle in the Henry Schmidt family war. Even the phone-perching Wenger twins had trouble stirring up much gossip. Edward R. Murrow would have ignored it entirely had it been in the European theater.

That January was particularly fierce, or maybe it just seemed that way because Emily and I walked to school every day, leaning into a biting wind in the morning and letting it push at our skirts and stockings on the way home in the afternoon. Our path took us past snapping flags that decorated porches like candy canes. Lots of houses had pictures—like a talisman—of sons or husbands in the windows, boys in marine, navy, or army dress, flight helmets or sailor suits, or sometimes simply in the neat suit and tie of a school picture. I was glad none of these folks ever drove out to our place to look for Ben's picture in the window. It wasn't there. They might confuse that to mean we didn't agonize over his safety as incessantly as these other families, but that wouldn't be true. If you measured agony in the number of sleepless hours, Mama would have come in first. Patriotism is a religion. Since we already had our own religion, Dad wouldn't let us put up the symbols of that one, even if one of the icons was a picture of his own son.

In February, President Roosevelt decided that telling us how much gas we could use wasn't enough. Now, he planned to limit the number of shoes we could buy each year. For good measure, he added canned goods and cheese to the rationing list, too. Now our arrangements with the Benders included some rationing coupons and canned beef from our cellar, which meant that Edwin could keep on having a paper thin slice of bacon at breakfast once a week. I don't think we shared any of our coffee coupons with them, though, because Edwin complained every morning about the Postum.

We had a lot less to complain about than the Germans, though, since they finally decided that invading Russia wasn't such a good idea after all. They surrendered at Stalingrad, a hundred thousand fewer than when they started the campaign, not counting those missing toes, feet, hands, and ears lost to frostbite and spirits lost to what they'd seen and done. Edwin, like Dad, never failed to include a request for peace in his prayers. That night, he thanked the good Lord that the Germans had finally come to their senses and asked for more of the same in France, Belgium, and Holland. The Japanese also needed a good dose of common sense in Asia, but they didn't know better and just kept battling to the death for every square inch of land, whether it was rightfully theirs or not. I think their plan was simply to wear us all down, which I feared they'd succeed at.

That Thursday, I dreamed my dream again about Mama, the one with the flowers and the letter from the War Department, Commanding General, Army Forces, Washington, saying that Ben is lost behind enemy lines. Only this time in my dream it's a white winter. The flowers boast no color except the rotten green of frozen vines and blooms. Mama's shaking the letter at God, who's nowhere to be seen. In the gray air behind Mama and the letter, I see Ben. He's leaning against the elm, his hand casually hanging onto the loop of a noose, which is how we all know he's going to die.

Adrenaline woke me. I was desperate to call Mama to warn her, but the dream was too complicated and at the same time, I felt too foolish. What would I warn her about? Dreams are dreams. Nothing more. But this dream came to breakfast with me that morning and sat beside me at school, poking me every time I tried to listen. On the way home, it pretended to be the wind, tapping me on the shoulder and whispering in my ear. When Dad picked me up, the dream hitched itself to the trunk and peered through the back window. All day, it waited patiently for me to break its spell by telling someone, and I couldn't.

I carried my bag into the house and set it down by the kitchen table where Mama stacked letters from Ben, Sam, Suzanne, and the occasional cousin. Suzanne—only two months past the unintended insults of my last visit and two months away from freedom—had all but stopped writing. Ben and Sam had both written. Ben's, because it was opened already, I read first. He'd seen Sam. They'd spent time with Sam's family and enjoyed a lively conversation about the best meals they'd ever eaten. With his usual dry wit, Ben said he felt sorry for Sam's family since the best meal they'd ever eaten included something called pasty pie and black pudding.

Sam, too, wrote about the time with Ben and how much he missed Mama's cherry cobbler. He said I should be practicing how to make that crunchy topping because when he got home, he wanted to eat that every day of his life. For two minutes, I forgot about the dream and fervently read between the lines.

This all reassured Mama. Not the part about me making the cherry cobbler, which I of course skipped over, but the fact that, once again, Sam saw Ben and he not only still had his humor, but he also still had his appendages. I wanted to shake Mama's shoulders. A three-week old letter didn't tell us what happened yesterday.

But people believe what they want to believe. And Mama, for all her flamingo qualities, wanted to believe that Ben was whole and sound and dreaming of her cherry cobbler, too.

That night, sleeping in my own bed, I thought I dreamed the dream again because I woke up to a rosy-cheeked Mama in the garden when she should have been frying eggs and mush downstairs. But it wasn't the dream. Instead, Mama bent under a stormy spring sky and sang "Rock of Ages, Cleft for Me" while she raked up leaves and cleaned off the rotted vines and leftover winter debris. The sun was still early on the horizon, and it pierced the gray clouds with lavender spears of light, giving them a drama they didn't deserve. Behind her in the direction of the pasture, the clouds hung lower, nearly kissing the ground. I could smell rain coming, that sweet spring kind that cleanses and revives and helps you love the earth more than money.

I pushed up my window and breathed it in. Mama heard the window. She looked up and smiled. "Good morning, Cat!" There was real joy in her voice.

"Good morning!"

"I couldn't help myself. I smelled the rain coming and the air felt warm for the first time in weeks. I was just itching to get out here. Don't you love that smell?" She breathed in deeply. Her hair was still loosely braided down her back, her night braid. From this distance, I couldn't see any gray in her hair. She looked ageless. "Give me just a few more minutes out here, and I'll come in and start breakfast."

I hesitated. For a foolish moment I wanted her to leave the garden so the dream wouldn't come true. There was no more logic to that, though, than the dream itself. "Stay out there and enjoy the morning. I'll make breakfast." I tried to freeze the moment forever in my head.

Then Mama turned her head to the sliver of road she could see from the garden. I couldn't see anything, but I heard the distant rattle of an engine. Mama looked back at me, her lower jaw slightly twisted, and I think we both realized at that moment we'd shared this dream. I threw on my Saturday clothes and a choring sweater and flew down the steps, stopping just outside on the steps of the summer porch. Mama still stood, frozen to the ground in the garden, rake and vines in hand, and watched the dark blue sedan pull into our lane. Dad stepped out of the barn, pushed his hat back, and scratched his forehead. I tried to see if he knew this dream, too, but he was too far away to read his eyes. How could he not have had this dream? For all that he and Ben scrapped, they loved each other. I knew it.

The government man stopped under the cottonwood and let the winter road dust catch up to him and settle. I could see him lift his hat, slick his hair back with one swipe of a hand, and readjust his hat. He stepped out of the sedan. He was wearing a green military suit and holding a white envelope. A suit on a Saturday morning on a Kansas farm. If you deliver funeral news, I guess you have to wear funeral clothes. Who would want this job? This job of telling people their boys were dead. What must *this* man dream about?

Mama still stood in the garden and Dad at the barn door, their wombs.

The man kept walking to the house, expecting to be a magnet to Dad. He knew his job well, or he didn't care and just wanted to put the envelope in someone's—anyone's—hand so he could leave and put the next envelope in the next someone's hand. At some moment, he must have looked at me and realized that I was too young to be a mother of a boy killed in the war. He shifted his path to Dad at the barn. If he saw Mama in the garden, he must have sensed not to go there. The man lifted his hat slightly and handed the envelope to Dad. He talked and nodded while Dad opened the envelope and read it. Then they both talked and nodded some more. The man shook Dad's hand, touched the brim of his green hat, and left.

Mama still stood in the garden, rake and vines in hand.

My throat felt fat and achy. Tears burned my eyes, but I didn't move.

Dad walked over to Mama in the garden and read the letter to her. I couldn't hear him, but I could see her. And then, for the first time in my life, I saw him embrace her. He held her and she held him, the dead vines still clutched in her hand. She buried her face in his chest, and her body shook with sobs.

The air grew heavier and thicker from mist. There would be no Ben and a noose by the elm tree because Ben was already gone. My legs and arms were lead.

Dad and Mama turned and walked toward the house. They kept on hanging on to each other, like one of them would fall if they let go. She kept sobbing and sobbing. Dad folded the letter and tucked it in between his shirt and overalls to keep it from the damp. Mama still carried the dead vines.

Where would we find flowers for her in February?

When they reached the house, Mama let go of Dad and wrapped her arms around me, hard.

"He's gone." She said between sobs.

"I know," I said, barely able to breathe or think. Our flesh and blood had been here in this house and now it never would be again.

"He was captured behind German lines. They don't know if he's dead or alive," Dad mumbled. His voice was thick and slurred.

"But he's not dead."

Dad shook his head. "They don't know. No one knows."

"Then that's good news. That he could still be alive." I felt blood tingling into my fingers and toes again.

We sat at the kitchen table and read the letter over and over out loud, looking for a word here, a word there that brought comfort. We hung our hopes on "captured alive." We couldn't feel any pride, though, in "your son's significant and courageous war contributions" because it only meant he had to have done something really horrible to be significant. This nonsense that "the entire nation shares your sorrow" seemed so false that I wanted to take a fountain pen and ink it out. President Roosevelt himself had signed the letter with a tilted, stamped signature that, sad to say, revealed his true callousness. I knew enough to know that he didn't sign—or stamp—just every boy's letter. That whispered lines between the lines to us. The president ended the letter with more empty phrases: "I send you my deepest sympathy in your hour of trial and pray that in Almighty God you will find the comfort and help that only He can bring."

In this household, that Almighty God was already mad at us that we'd let one of His children go off and kill more of His children. I didn't think he'd be in a comforting mood. And frankly, I wasn't sure he thought we deserved any different.

When Kenny Kistle disappeared on the Bataan Peninsula, we'd said not knowing was worse than knowing. But now that it was Ben I didn't believe it. Not knowing meant that Ben could still be alive. The letter said "captured alive," so we had to believe that he could still be alive.

Dad and I found the tiniest bit of hope in that. But Mama couldn't. "That's my heart walking around out there." She spread her hand over her heart as if to hold it in. I remembered the floured handprint on her apron when the war swallowed up Kenny Kistle somewhere on the tip of the Philippines.

"And he still may be alive." We almost pleaded with her.

She shook her head and whispered through her sobs. "If he's a prisoner, he'll suffer. He's all alone, abandoned. What deaths will he long for?" Mist clung to her hair and sweater. Or maybe she'd already cried that much. "And what if he truly is dead, and we've cleaved to this hope? Then I'll have died two deaths." She buried her head in her hands and sobbed.

As much as we all wanted Ben to be alive, I knew Mama's agony. Having the tiniest shoot of hope that he was alive and to live on that only to find out a week, a month—a year—later that he was dead after all would be the cruelest trick of all. And what if we never found out? What if the war dragged on for decades? What if Stalingrad was only a blip in the German war machine and now they had new resolve? Or what if they really had some secret weapon that would destroy our will to fight, this secret that only Kansas farmers knew enough to whisper about at the co-op, but Edward R. Murrow never dared tell us about? Would it be worse for him to be alive and molding in some German prisoner of war camp for decades? Was it fair to want him to suffer—alive, yes—but endure intense pain and sickness of the heart just so that someday we could have maybe only his hollow shell back? Would it be better to lose him and remember him as he was than to have him return broken and twisted like that Plett boy who brought his ghosts back from World War I? Which was more selfish?

Maybe Mama was being the most generous of us all to say let him be dead. Mama and her flamingo ways.

Dad helped Mama to her room, where she just stayed. I fried us all some eggs and toasted some bread, but Mama's just grew cold on the plate on her bedstand. Dad was lost. He picked up the phone several times and then set it down. We were so conditioned not to let the party line know our sorrows that even now, he just couldn't bring himself to make a phone call. Finally, he put on his hat and told me he was going into town to let Edwin and Tilly know. It was worth the coupons of gas to him.

I had the house to myself for four long hours. I cleaned for a while, mostly swiping the dust on the furniture and floors because no matter the time of year, Kansas always insists on coming inside, and I started zwieback and cinnamon rolls so the house would smell like a Saturday. Something had to seem the same. Outside, the clouds dropped lower and lower, enveloping the farm. Was God trying to comfort us after all?

Finally, I sat down to write letters. It was a Sunday activity on a Saturday, but that day would also be mixed up. On the first piece of paper, I began, *Dear Ben,* then immediately crumpled up the paper, horrified that my fingers could forget so quickly. I started over, this time with a salutation to Sam. Only a paragraph followed. He would understand. I ended with my usual *come home safely,* but the words seemed like an empty magic incantation. I wrote to Suzanne, too, but I worried that instead of caring, she would sneer slightly, relieved that the Peterses were finally carrying a burden as great as the Schmidts.

Dad still wasn't back, so I started writing short notes to the aunts and uncles. Mama might bring herself to write to them later, but this way they would know within a week or two. There was something cathartic about this.

Ben has been captured. He's missing behind German lines. We don't know if he's dead or alive. Keep us in your prayers.

Please keep us in your prayers.

I wrote it over and over and over. I cried while I wrote, but the tingling stayed and the numbness didn't return, so I knew it was the thing I should do.

Finally, I wrote a note to Mrs. Kistle. I didn't have her address, but Rural Route, Pratt, would get it to her eventually. I knew of all the people I wrote to that day—maybe even Sam—she would know and understand the best.

When Dad finally came home, he had a card and two pies that Tilly had magically whipped up and six red roses in a vase.

"Red roses! Where in the world did you find those?"

"I drove on over to Dodge. They have one of those flowers stores over there." He looked a little sheepish, but his eyes were swollen and red.

He'd spent how many more gas coupons and good money on real flowers. The extravagance made my heart soar. Maybe it would touch Mama's heart in the same way and we wouldn't lose her along with Ben after all.

"Ezra!" was all she could say. But she actually laughed through her tears. We closed the door to the bedroom and hoped the scent could settle into the corners and weave itself into the bedding and curtains. Maybe it would dull the pain.

Late afternoon, while Dad was still out choring, I heard horse hooves padding in the barnyard. It surprised me that Dad would get on a horse and ride, but maybe that somehow reminded him of Ben and brought him the same kind of comfort that flowers brought Mama.

A while later, the horse hooves padded in the barnyard again. A few minutes later Dad came inside carrying a kettle. He handed me the still-warm kettle and washed up.

"What's this?" I asked, thoroughly confused.

He took off his hat and jacket and soaped up. He pointed at the kettle with his chin. "Open it."

It was a roasted chicken and potatoes that smelled as good as the roses at that moment. "Who brought this?" I hadn't heard a car.

"Henry."

"Henry Schmidt?"

Dad nodded and dried his hands. "He brought it just now. Rode his horse over."

"Because of Ben?"

"Think about it, Cat. Who else in this church knows better what it means to have lost a child." His voice sounded as thick as it did when he handed me the letter from the War Department.

"It's not the same at all. He was the one who caused his daughters to leave." I sounded like the Schmidt girls. How easy it is to be on both sides of the coin.

"Don't mean that it didn't destroy him."

"But that's what he deserved."

"Is it? Is this what I deserve because I didn't let Ben go to that state university and play basketball like he wanted?" His eyes watered. Had he been carrying that guilt all this time?

"It's not the same. Not the same at all," I said, and gritted my teeth.

"Isn't it? You never know what a body'd choose to do different if he just had a chance."

CHAPTER 10

We knew the good Lord would have wanted us in church that Sunday, but none of us could go twenty minutes without tearing up, which wouldn't even take us within striking range of the sermon. Besides, we couldn't take the staring, however sympathetic. For the first time in my entire life, the three of us skipped church without being sick. Well, that's not entirely accurate because the three of us were very heartsick. Just because a body isn't running a fever or throwing up their insides doesn't mean they're not too sick to be around other people.

That afternoon, Edwin and Tilly came calling, along with what seemed like half the church. They brought food, cards, tears, stories, and Norma Miller, bless her heart, a potted geranium she'd been nurturing through the winter. Mama came out of her rose-scented mausoleum periodically, but sometimes the ladies just went to her bedroom and sat with her there. If anyone thought that we got what we'd deserved for having a boy who was a cog in that giant war machine, they had the courtesy not to say it or not to stop by in the first place.

Mama let me stay home from school that week. God forgave us for not going to church and gave us gentle temperatures and sweet nighttime rains every day. We cleaned up the vegetable garden and flowerbeds. On Wednesday, we squandered even more gas coupons and drove past greening winter wheat fields and pastures all the way to Greensburg, bypassing Sweethome, where we'd see too many people we knew, to buy seeds and a rose bush.

The lady at the counter asked if we were planting a Victory garden. Mama and I got the giggles of all goofy things, so Dad just said yes, that's exactly what we were doing. For too many years it had been a survival garden and this week it was a save-Mama's-sanity garden. But if it made the United States government happy and it gave us a better chance that Ben would come home, we'd call it a Victory garden. Dad even tooted the V for Victory honk—dot, dot, dot, dash—on the way out of the parking lot.

Maybe we were one of them now.

We stopped at Mercy's Cafe because of the name and had a meatloaf, corn, and mashed potato dinner with chocolate chiffon pie and coffee for the three of us. It was a decadent meal, one that didn't cost a single ration coupon except for all the gas to get there and back. I didn't know when we were going to stop hemorrhaging money and gas coupons, but that wasn't the question of the day, so I just tried to live in the moment and be grateful that Dad had a dollar in his pocket and a car to take us away from our misery for a few hours.

When we got home, we worked in the garden the rest of the day. Dad and I planted peas, lettuce, radishes, red potatoes, sweet potatoes, turnips, and onion sets and got the rest of it tilled up for the seeds that would wait for warmer weather. Mama fussed around the flower beds, creating a special spot for Ben's rose bush, as she called it, so she could see it from the kitchen window and from the car when we drove into the lane. As long as we were outside, she had color in her cheeks.

On Friday, the postal service played a cruel war trick on us and delivered a letter from Ben. We should have been expecting it since even though his letters had been more sporadic since he'd been shipped—like a package, not a person—overseas, the letters still came. Still, none of us could open it at first. Worse, we knew another one could come from him next week, and maybe one after that as well.

The letter sat on the kitchen table, Ben's tilted scrawl staring at us, teasing us, pretending that everything was okay. By opening the letter, we would momentarily live in two times: the one where Ben was alive and safe and making silly jokes about who snored the loudest in his barrack and this one, where we knew the truth and the pain ran deep like a gorge through every waking minute.

Finally, after supper, Mama made three cups of real coffee and opened a jar of canned peaches. She poured a little cream and sprinkled some cinnamon on the peaches. Dad slit open the tissue-thin mail gram with his pocketknife and read it out loud.

"My dearest family," Dad read. Color rose in his weathered cheeks and his mouth twitched once or twice. He cleared his throat and began again.

My dearest family.

I just received three letters from you. It felt like Christmas! I keep reading them over and over. Each time I hear your voices and it makes me wish I could see your faces and reach out and touch you. Wish I could see some good old Kansas sunshine, too. Some of the boys are laying bets around here how many days we can go without seeing the sun. Don't worry, Mama, I haven't picked up that vice yet. (I'm waiting for the stakes to go higher. Ha! Ha!) All that rain surely makes things green around here. Including the skin between my toes! Ha! I don't know if I'll ever dry out!

I'm sorry to hear that Marie Schmidt died. It seemed fast didn't it? Or maybe it was because I'm here, so far away from things. It's odd in a way. It seems like every week someone I know doesn't come back from a mission. I know death better than a twenty-one-year old boy should ever know it—

Dad stopped reading and blew his nose on his bandana. Mama sipped at her coffee and stared at the table.

—but Marie's death hit me in a different way. I guess it was because I've known those Schmidt girls longer than I've been walking and talking and I could only imagine

what it must be like for them to lose their mama. How are they taking it? Suzanne and Dess write every now and then, but I haven't heard from either of them since this news. Mama, I'm sure glad I still have you!

Mama cleared her throat and we all stopped to wipe our eyes.

Did I write you that Sam and I met for supper last week? He surely is a likable fellow. He was sporting captain's bars this time. That's a pretty fine promotion for no longer than he's been in. He'll probably be too modest to write you that himself. You'll have to razz him about it when you write him again. Anyway, we've agreed that it's swell that Dodge City and Sweethome are so close together. He's one fellow I'll want to stay in touch with after this thing is over.

My heart pounded. Ben could have been writing all that pretty innocently, but I didn't think so. Knowing Ben, there was a message there for me.

The other boys are headed to the mess hall, so I should be going. Someone said we've got some roast beef tonight. Hope it was one of our cows! The last time we had roast beef someone must have switched the shipment with a crate of old shoes. Ha! They said just throw a little more catsup on it. Except they didn't have any catsup either. Must have gotten switched with a shipment of canned spinach, which there seems to be no end of. I don't think that spinach had seen a garden in two years!

Hope the wheat's looking good. Take care of yourselves. Don't worry about me. I'm safe and sound. I'm eating good (except for the spinach and the shoes they pass off as roast beef) and sleeping in a nice warm bed every night.

Your loving son and brother, Ben.

Nothing. There was nothing at all that hinted about what was to come, no shadows, no silhouettes, just the words that said "don't worry, I'm fine." How many other times had he shaken hands with death only to walk away? He had stories. He'd alluded to that often enough for us to know. They were stories that he knew would give us restless nights and heavy hearts, so he wrote about roast beef and weather and growing mold between his toes.

The letter made me angry that he didn't trust us with his fears. Now that we knew the worst, I hated his lies about being safe and sound. We'd known all along that they were only partially true—he *did* disappear into the inky night of the war periodically—but now they weren't just lies, they were insults. He didn't believe we could hear the truth.

For the first time in a week, I felt something other than knife-sharp, devastating loss. Oddly enough, it lifted my spirits, more because it felt different than because it felt good.

The three of us kept stumbling through our weeks. I kept going home with the Benders on Sunday and returning home on Friday, spending the week in between letting my legs carry me on their familiar route from class to class, hoping that enough Latin, chemistry, and English could still seep into my brain and I could graduate in May with my grades more or less intact. Dad fretted even more than other years about the wheat, the rain, and the price of hogs. I guess all that seemed more controllable than what might have happened to Ben. And Mama struggled something fierce every day just to get up, pull a comb through her hair, and put something on the table for us to eat. Dad said she spent a lot of hours in the garden, but it looked to me like she wandered more than she tilled.

Some weeks after we heard about Ben, Mrs. Kistle arrived with a kettle of food and a cherry pie. She'd had Kermit skip school—a great burden to him, I'm sure—and drive her over. Mama told me on Saturday she'd been overwhelmed by the generosity of the food and the gas. Mrs. Kistle had been surprisingly comforting. They could cry together and name their fears. Mrs. Kistle followed that visit with at least one card or letter every week, signing each one, "Your sister in Christ." She might have been, but more important at the moment, she was Mama's sister in sadness.

That spring, Mama would have been happy to be a Catholic because she could have gone to church and lit a candle for Ben every single day, gas rationing or not. But we weren't Catholic and we didn't have good symbols, so she finally at least put Ben's picture up in our window, even though no one would see it but us and our church friends who came calling. Even the postman wouldn't see it unless he delivered a box, which happened so few times a year that I knew the picture wasn't for him. It was a basketball picture, one that the *Sweethome Tribune* had taken the winter before he left, and it seemed more fitting than his senior picture where he looked soberly into the camera with the expression of a boy trapped in a suit coat and tie.

The talisman brought us another letter from Ben before he was captured and two other letters that were hard to read. The first came from Sam in mid March but was written in late February.

He wrote,

> *I probably shouldn't worry you with this, but Ben and I were supposed to meet last Thursday for supper and he didn't show. I know he has duties that take him lots of places, but he's always been able to get word to me and this time he didn't. He probably had a flat tire some place. Happens all the time what with the lousy tires and all the metal shrapnel on the roads. I'm just surprised that he's never sent a message about it. It isn't like him. Well, the good news is that by the time you get this, the two of us will have had supper a couple of times and this will be just a small joke between us.*

There wasn't any good news. There wouldn't be any small jokes.

The second letter, from a fellow named Ernie Kowalski, came a week or so later on a Saturday, so I was home when it arrived. We didn't know any Ernie Kowalski, but it had a military return address that looked like Ben's. We studied the mail gram and talked about what could be in it for a good hour and fifteen minutes before we decided to open it and read it. We finally agreed that if it was solid news that Ben was dead, it wouldn't come this way. Surely, they'd send a government man out to tell us. How could any other news be worse than that?

We decided we could read the letter. Mama cut three slices of a cherry pie she'd made for church potluck the next day. She made three cups of coffee—real coffee—an emerging sign that the world could end soon, so there would be no need to ration the rations. We sat at the kitchen table while Dad carefully sliced open the top of the mail gram and smoothed it flat.

> *Dear Mr. and Mrs. Peters and Cat,*
>
> *Even though we've never met, I've heard so much about all of you that it feels like I'm writing to my own family. Ben and I have been in the same unit, almost since the beginning, and he feels like a brother to me. When I heard the news about him and the other boys being captured, I felt sicker than words could say. He didn't deserve this. Not that anyone ever does, but Ben of all people was too good of a boy.*

The sentence hung. Was too good of a boy for what? Capture? Torture? Certain death? The wrath of God? What didn't he deserve?

Dad cleared his throat and took a sip of coffee. He began again.

I have to tell you that he's the finest young man I've had the privilege of knowing. He was honest, kind, caring, and genuine. Most of all though, I'd never met someone with as much integrity. I know he was troubled with being in the midst of all of this. We all are, but he was in a different way. We talked about this lots. Like the rest of us, he knew firsthand the horrors of what we were fighting and was committed to ending it, yet there was something in him that made him keep asking if there wasn't a better way.

He struggled with the importance of what he was doing and at the same time, what he saw as the wrongness of it. He confided in me that he made a conscious decision at some point to fight this evil, even if he lost part of his own soul doing it. The two of us didn't necessarily see eye to eye on this, but there isn't a boy I have more respect for. He understands the price he's paying, and he's chosen this path fully conscious of it.

I wish I could reassure you that Ben will be okay. I can't, and I don't want to give you false hopes. I'm told he was captured alive and, as far as anyone knows, not injured. We know he'll suffer. It's the nature of war. But he has an inner strength and a belief in the Almighty God that will carry him. Have faith.

In closing, I have to tell you about a pact that Ben and I made. If something ever happened to him, he wanted me to write to his family. He said to tell you that 'this is more important than basketball.' I'm not sure what this is all about but I do know this surely is more important than basketball.

Someday, when this is all over . . . and I have faith that it will be all over someday, I hope to meet you and share stories with you about Ben.

God bless you,
Ernie Kowalski.

The letter was supposed to calm us somehow and make us believe there was purpose to our loss. I guess we were supposed to feel proud of Ben, too. Instead, we had to sort through all the unsaid things—what had he seen firsthand? What were the horrors he knew? How would he suffer? "The nature of war," that's how Ernie Kowalski excused it.

Worst of all, though, the words were on paper. He'd given up part of his soul to fight this evil. He knew what he'd done. This was no more the defiant lark of a rebellious boy.

We crept deeper into our despair, helped along by this boy's kind words.

CHAPTER 11

APRIL THAT YEAR BROUGHT EASTER and Suzanne's release from her sentence. It should have been a time of repentance, forgiveness, and new beginnings, but it wasn't because those are all things a body has to choose.

The rest of us practiced the rituals of the season: footwashing and communion. Neither one was the right one to fill the holes in the hearts of Dad, Mama, and me. There wasn't a religion on earth that could do that. But we all drank the grape juice and broke the bread and became servants—at least for five minutes—while we washed someone else's feet. The rite was intended to mimic Christ when he was the guest of honor but became a servant and washed his followers' feet: the powerful washing the feet of the powerless. That would have meant that Ethel should have been doing some serious footwashing, but I don't think she even came to church that night. Consciously or subconsciously, she understood the symbolism. Isn't that always the case? The folks standing in the most need of prayer are the ones home reading *Capper's Weekly*.

Henry Schmidt came, though, looking ragged and sallow. He took communion, so he must have been feeling washed in the blood and in a state of grace. He paired up with Earl Yoder, the oldest, most myopic, most deaf resident of the amen corner for the footwashing. They had a safe conversation, I'm sure.

Suzanne traded her brown dresses for a new civilian dress and rode the bus to Sweethome, where she spent a week with Tim, Inez, Dess, and Moses. Emily just skipped school that week and stayed with Inez and all. They invited me to come for the weekend so I could see Suzanne before she got back on a bus headed for Wichita and the Boeing airplane factory.

I couldn't go, though. I wanted to see Suzanne, but I wanted it to be short and I didn't want it to be in the land of the Schmidt sisters where the opportunities would be ripe for saying all the wrong things. Tilly Bender solved the whole problem. She invited Dad and Mama and the entire Schmidt brood—minus Henry of course—to supper on Friday. Except for Betsy and Pete, it was a trip we all would have made anyway, so no one had to feel guilty about the gas.

Now we Mennonites entertained all the time, but unless you were a visiting distant cousin, missionary, harvest helper, or a hobo passing through, the entertaining always took place on a Sunday, either at noon after church—which frequently carried you all the way to supper time—or in the evening after church for a bowl of homemade ice cream or popcorn. Inviting local folks for supper on a Friday somehow seemed to twist up everyone's week. No one knew quite how to dress, and poor Tilly didn't know quite what food to fix. You just couldn't turn leftover hash into company fare no matter how many eggs you added or how much catsup you poured on it. And a month of ration coupons wouldn't buy enough roast or chickens to feed the lot, so she opted for meatloaf with enough breadcrumbs to stretch it nearly beyond recognition.

Tilly had me set the table with her good china, so I was glad that Dad and Mama at least arrived in their Sunday clothes, no easy thing since they would have had to rush through choring to get there on time. Tim and Inez and all showed up promptly at six, cleaned and pressed but in a weekday assortment of overalls and dresses.

I'd worried all week about the awkwardness of those first few minutes with Suzanne. Would we fling our arms around each other and hug? Would we coolly smile and nod at each other from across the room? Would one of us—probably me since I lived constantly close to tears these days—cry? What had we done when I went to visit her? I couldn't remember.

When the moment came, she didn't hesitate. She threw her arms around me and hugged me tight. She laughed like the old Suzanne used to, the one I knew before we'd both lost our childhoods. Her curly hair was short and bouncy, and her eyes crinkled tight when she smiled. She sparkled, really. It wasn't what I'd expected given how gray her emotions had been when I visited her in jail. As the evening wore on, though, I realized she was a July radish: all red and pretty on the outside, but bitter and wooden on the inside.

We waited for Betsy, Pete, and their three ragamuffins to show up, but they must not have had the gas coupons to come or a phone to cancel. Or the presence of mind to show up. Their five plates stared at us for a good half hour before Inez started clearing them and distracting us with a funny story about Moses and his discovery of where eggs came from. Once again, I was glad Tilly hadn't made hash.

We finally sat down to eat and almost immediately realized there wasn't a safe conversation to have. We couldn't talk about church because half the folks at the table had stomped out years ago. We couldn't talk about Suzanne and her last two years of incarceration because it would have been fiercely rude. And we couldn't talk about the war because two of us would burst into tears and a third would go into a coughing fit and have to step out on the back porch. This meant we also couldn't talk about anything rationed or in short supply—which now included every corner of our lives: food, shoes, bubblegum, tires, metal toys, dish soap, paper, toothpaste, rubber dolls, and baseballs. We could hardly even talk about gardening or the price of beef because one way or another, they'd all lead to our boys overseas, which would lead us back to our hankies. Instead we talked about the weather and the meatloaf and Moses as much as he would let us.

After supper, Tilly excused Suzanne and me from dish duty. The two of us drifted out to the front porch and settled on the swing. A cool, bold wind had blustered us all day, but now it was done and the evening settled soft and warm. Even though it neared eight o'clock, oranges and pinks hung in the sky and wrapped us with the smell of spring. Cicadas sang to us.

We pushed ourselves back and forth for a while in silence. I felt awkward. It seemed like we should have had a hundred things to chatter about, but I couldn't find any way to start into them, especially because I didn't want to be cut by the many sharp edges she'd grown while in jail. Finally, Suzanne began. "My room was on the east side of the building. I didn't see a sunset for almost two years."

"How terrible!" It sounded insincere and trite, but I meant it. What do you say to someone who missed two years of sunsets? Sometimes that's the only good part of the day.

She shrugged her shoulders like it didn't matter anymore.

"Do you know anything more about Ben?"

I locked my jaw and waited for the inevitable tears. I shook my head.

Suzanne leaned her head against the swing chain and looked at me. "Prison isn't always that bad. I told myself every day that it was better than being at Simon Yoder's and better than living with Pops."

I had to breathe deeply and consciously before I talked again. "I don't think he would say the same thing about his situation."

She shrugged one shoulder. "Maybe not."

We rocked some more. Evening shadows stretched down the street, draping houses and cars in grays, then blacks. A block over, children noises filled the air. Shrieks, laughter, high-pitched voices. "Ollie, ollie over!"

"No matter what, he'll come back changed. You know that, don't you?"

"Of course, I know that. I just want him to come back."

"And I hope if he comes back, you still feel that way."

I could hear my heart thumping in my ears, and my palms felt damp. True or not, it wasn't the sort of thing a friend should ever say to a friend. I was glad when the evening finally ended and she could go off to her Boeing airplane plant in Wichita.

CHAPTER 12

Y OU'D HAVE THOUGHT THAT A government that had the wherewithal to build over a hundred thousand tanks and nearly three hundred and twenty-five thousand airplanes during the war would have had the common sense not to remind a mama on Mother's Day that her son was lost behind enemy lines. But apparently not. The good old U.S. of A. Army shipped us Ben's trunk of things to arrive on Saturday, the day before Mother's Day.

The trunk—unexpected and unwanted—should never have come to us. The army would have been better off pushing it overboard somewhere in the middle of the Atlantic. Sending it so promptly didn't make us marvel at their efficiency as much as confirm our suspicions that they only saw Ben as one more boy with a pulse to put in front of the cannons. And now his things were in the way. At the very least, they should have waited six months to send it so they'd appear hopeful. Like us.

Mama was in her flowerbed, of course, fussing around the peonies, which had bloomed early that year, when

George Andons brought the trunk out from town. He ran a small freight company, so it wasn't his fault that he brought the trunk out to the farm. And it wasn't really Mama's fault that she never forgave him, forever referring to him as "that man George who brought Ben's trunk out to the farm" and ignoring not only had she known him and his heart of gold for twenty-some years, but for heaven's sakes this was what he was paid to do. I'd studied Mr. Pavlov and his dogs, so I at least had half a brain about how a body would connect one with the other, even if the stimulus only happened one time.

Poor George thought he'd brought something good for us, something left over from our boy. But George was a Catholic, who smoked by the way, and didn't understand we'd had two horrible losses, not just one. George had lost his own boy in a bombing run in 1943 over some unpronounceable locale in Western Germany, so he thought we were the same. George was sad but proud to give up his son to this good fight. We, on the other hand, had lost Ben, first to everything that Dad, Mama, and I stood for, and then to death, maybe, itself. We figured, in fact, that was what the army was telling us by sending us the trunk: your boy's dead, here's his stuff, don't write.

George hefted the battered black metal trunk into the kitchen where we walked around the thing all morning. It wasn't exactly as if opening it would seal Ben's fate, but we also certainly couldn't treat it like a Christmas package. When he'd last latched it, he'd planned to return. Would Ben have straightened out his things just in case he'd never come back? What if he unknowingly left something that would further destroy our memory of him?

We couldn't open it. Instead, after dinner, we toted the trunk up to Ben's old room and left it by the bed, under the window, in the same room where his clothes, schoolbooks, basketball, and scrapbook of basketball clippings and pictures had stayed untouched. It sat above us, somber, heavy, and soundless, and carried a shadow that slithered through all the rooms and even through the windows out into the garden, taking our hearts with it. Mama, who in the last few weeks had begun to revive again, cell by cell, as spring came on, now returned to her darkened bedroom. She couldn't come out on Saturday evening for supper, so I carried a tray and a giant bouquet of lilacs into her room and sat by her bed, coaxing her to sit up, brush her hair, take a bite.

"Fetch Ben's letters out of my top dresser drawer, Cat."

I dutifully retrieved the letters.

"Read them to me, would you?"

I quaked inside. Just seeing his choring cap on the hook on the summer porch could make me cry. I didn't want to spend the rest of the evening reading his handwriting and turning my insides out, knowing now like we did that this wasn't even his real world. "Do you really think that's a good idea?"

She didn't answer me. Except for the trunk that had begun to whisper to us from the next room, it was quiet.

Reluctantly, I untied the red ribbon that had been tied and untied so often that it had feathery edges all along it.

The letters were ordered chronologically: from boot camp to England.

"Dear Family." Tears blurred the tilted lines of ink and my head felt too full to talk. I blew my nose. "Why do you want to read these now?" I asked her softly.

"This is all we might have of him. I think I've already forgotten his voice."

"But these letters aren't him. These aren't the real Ben. He lied to us, Mama. Doesn't that hurt?"

"It doesn't matter. I love him. Nothing changes that."

I tried to read again, but couldn't finish a line without blowing my nose. "I can't do this."

"Then let me just hold the letters."

I folded the one I was reading and put it back in the envelope and tied the ribbon around the stack. She shouldn't have used a red ribbon.

"He's my flesh and blood." The sound came from her mouth, but it was thin and flat, not Mama's voice at all. She wasn't crying, but I'm not sure why not unless she'd drained her reservoir. Finally she looked at me instead of the wall. "I don't think he's dead. I think he's sad, sadder than the three of us together if you can imagine. But I think I'd know if his heart had stopped."

Although there was great pain in Mama's idea, it was still less pain than thinking he was dead somewhere, piled with others in a shallow, unmarked grave that maybe he'd had to help dig himself. There were always rumors about these sorts of things. Dad and I let ourselves pretend that Mama somehow knew. Mama and her flamingo vision. I don't know if we were better or worse off with this idea, but it was the one we planted, watered, and nurtured.

I went home with the Benders that Sunday evening and all week tried not to think about what was in the trunk. But it whispered to me all day long and stole into my dreams at night, weaving them with Germans who only laughed and laughed and coffin-sized trunks overflowing with cockroaches and crickets. I knew we needed to open it, no matter what we found or how final our goodbye to him would be.

Ignoring something like that only gives it power over you.

Not surprisingly, when I got home on Friday, Dad and Mama hadn't touched the trunk. But then, I don't suppose Mama had even been out of her room much.

"I think we should open it," I said at supper that night. We hadn't been talking about the trunk, but there was only one "it" that any of us had thought about all week.

Mama shook her head and teared up.

"I think we should. We don't have to do anything with his things, but we should know what his life consisted of for these last few years."

Dad stiffened. His mouth twitched slightly.

Mama shook her head more. "I can't. Not yet."

I looked at Dad, who mostly just looked at his bowl of ham-and-green-bean soup.

"Then I'll open it by myself and see what's in it." These words look defiant on paper, but I didn't say them that way. Neither Dad nor Mama said anything, which was the same thing as saying go ahead.

I cleaned up the supper dishes and made the ritual real coffee—three cups, even though Mama and Dad would be drinking theirs at the kitchen table and I'd be upstairs. It would have been nice to have had something a little sweet with the coffee, but pie had become far too frivolous. Unfortunately, not having something usually makes you want it more even if it was something you easily lived without before, so all of us lived with that tiny craving every day.

I cracked open the bottom half of Ben's window a few inches and let a little more of the evening in. It had started to rain, a soft spring rain and not a summer thunderstorm. It was the right way for the evening to smell—sweet and earthy against the bitter coffee. I sat cross-legged in front of the trunk, sipping the hot coffee, drinking in the mingled scents, deciding whether it really would be better not to know. Finally, I knew nothing as small as this trunk should ever keep me from getting on with life.

It was a good lesson to learn.

For all of our uneasiness, though, we knew little more about Ben afterwards than we did before. I expected the trunk to be packed tight. Three years of living can't help but take some room. But this one still had room enough for even more years in the army. Most of what the trunk held I expected. What I couldn't figure out was where the unexpected things were.

There were his clothes: one clean, neatly pressed officer's uniform; two sets of everyday army clothes; socks, undershirts, undershorts, and pajamas; his Sunday suit, shirt, and tie; a pair of tan dungarees; and a couple of carefully folded shirts.

He also had spit-shined-to-the-hilt boots and dress shoes and his basketball shoes that looked like he'd worn them considerably more than his Sunday suit.

The personal things included stacks of letters from Mama and me (and six from Dad), tied with a girl's blue hair ribbon; a much smaller stack of letters from others, mostly Dess Schmidt, but some from Suzanne, some cousins, and friends from church and school—again tied with a girl's hair ribbon; pictures of two unknown girls, one of whom had very awkward teeth; a German/English handbook; and a small box with some souvenir-kinds of things—pins, knickknacks, a dried rose. There were no newspaper clippings with Ben's byline, so even if we'd been willing to deceive ourselves before that he was some kind of reporter for the army newspaper, we had to stop. He wasn't any journalist.

It seemed so little that it felt like surely something was missing. Where were his books and writing things? He couldn't spell, but he certainly could—and did—read. The trunk seemed cleaned out, like someone had sanitized it, taken the secrets out of it, and made it safe for his family to view. It was as empty of Ben as his letters.

I made a list of the things and put them all back into the truck as much like I'd found them as I could. It could stay here now, along with all his other things that hadn't been touched, even to be dusted, since the telegram day.

That whole spring we'd carried stones in our stomachs thinking about what might have happened to Ben. Now the stones turned to boulders, to mountains. I was lucky the teachers thought I was smart because there wasn't a single thing I did or said between early March and graduation day to prove it, weighed down like I was about Ben.

For that matter, my whole class lived that spring with a nervous energy. In weeks or days after our graduation ceremony, we'd all be forced to grow up as the boys scattered off to the war machine that chewed up whole, healthy bodies and left aching holes behind. The Allies and the Axis had this awful teeter-totter game going: the Allies finally wrested control of Africa from the Axis; the Germans crushed an uprising in the Warsaw Jewish ghetto. The Germans had surrendered at Stalingrad, but increased U-boat activity, blowing up ships in the harbor of Halifax, Nova Scotia. Even though it was two thousand miles away and in another country, we touched the same land. They were the fingers of this body, which shuddered nervously with the assault.

Some of the boys in our class wouldn't come home. Soldiers died every day, maybe not as many, but the telegraph office still did too good of a business. Not all the boys in the class would carry a gun, though. Buddy Holmes, who had a game leg because of a surprise encounter with a threshing machine, got a 4F classification, which meant he wasn't fit enough to be in the army, even to peel potatoes at Camp Carson, Colorado. Most boys hated the classification because it labeled them as a cripple or weakling. But I can tell you right now that Mrs. Tilman Holmes, Buddy's mama, thanked the good Lord every day that what had seemed a tragedy at the time turned into a blessing. That's another good lesson in life.

The other boys who wouldn't be marching off to war were the Mennonite boys, who were headed into Civilian Public Service, or C.P.S. While Buddy had to suffer through the sissy jokes, the Mennonite boys heard all the coward, yellow belly, and Kraut slurs. Mr. Willis, the government teacher threatened to flunk any boy with a CO—conscientious objector—status, which would have meant they couldn't have graduated. While Mr. Willis would have benefited a little more from reading his own textbook, it was Mr. Tully, the former drill-sergeant-turned-shop teacher who came to their rescue. He not only defended them, he even sounded a tiny bit sympathetic to them.

None of them talked much about where they were headed, Buddy because he felt sheepish and the Mennonite boys because everyone thought they should feel sheepish and they didn't. Robert Miller carried his letter around in his pocket for two months without saying a word. He'd volunteered to go work in a mental hospital out in New Jersey. It wasn't a life-threatening sort of assignment, but was more akin to tending society's abandoned trash, so the job had a tendency to taint a body. Back then, mental hospitals and prisons drew from the same labor pool, a complicated arrangement because more than a few times, the folks doing the guarding traded places with the ones being guarded. Robert didn't tell many of the other boys and girls he was headed there.

He told me, though, the evening we had the baccalaureate service—the one where they preached to us the Sunday before they handed us our diplomas and graduated us.

We were all milling around in the hall, waiting to line up alphabetically for the second to the last time. The Reverend Oscar Moss from the Sweethome Living Waters Bible Church was delivering the sermon that night, and all the Living Waters Bible Church boys and girls were rolling their eyes and saying he'd be wagging his finger at us for a long dry evening and it wasn't fair since he'd wagged his finger at them all morning, too. I think the churches kind of rotated through the baccalaureate responsibilities from year to year since each of the churches needed a fair chance to do the sending. Having said this, though, I'm not sure if they ever invited the Mennonites to preach the sermon, and given the disdain most folks in town had for our peace stance, I'm not sure they'd even let Brother Bender pray since the late '30s. Under the circumstances, he would have had a hard time doing it right for most folks' theology, so it was probably just as well. During the war years, whoever prayed or preached depended heavily on the Old Testament and all those passages about battles where God was on the side of the Jews who destroyed the Philistines. They pretty much ignored the New Testament and all the scriptures that said things like "blessed are the peacemakers" and "love your neighbor as yourself."

It's human nature to pick out the verses that support what you're already doing and ignore the ones that make you uneasy, but some folks had awfully thin Bibles those years.

M for Miller and P for Peters would be a dozen bodies apart in a school of any size, but at Sweethome, just Lester Norb and Millie Ollert stood between Robert and me. If the

Kistles had still lived on the old Hallsey place, Kermit would have been in line on just the other side of Robert. Although probably not since in one of Mrs. Kistle's letters, she sobbed to Mama that Kermit had "took off and joined up" even though she'd begged him to at least wait till he was graduated from high school. Lester and Millie were off flirting with each other, fixing, I guess, to get engaged before Lester took off for the marines. A Kansas boy on a boat. Now *that* was the talk of the town.

Robert tilted his head toward giggling Millie. "Ever wonder how many folks get married just because they spend twelve years lining up next to each other?"

We small-talked a few minutes about what my plans were after graduation. In another year, a girl my age would teach school or work in a store until she got married. I might have done that too except for that little suggestion seed from Sam that I'd carefully carried inside me for six or seven months and now was a small tree that had taken root. Maybe some way, somehow, I'd figure out how to go to college and then on to law school. But I didn't dare share that with Robert—the college part or the Sam James part and certainly not the James & James part—even though I knew he could keep a secret. Instead I smiled and shrugged my shoulders and said, "Hard to know until the war's over. All I know is that it won't involve farming."

He laughed and shook his head. "At least we both learned something from surviving the last ten years."

The conversation slipped onto safer ground. We compared notes about where different boys were headed come the end of May and which ones had snagged a girl to come home to.

"I'm not even headed overseas, but I understand how having a girl back home makes it easier to leave."

I probably flushed a little. There would have been a time I would have been thrilled to be that girl; Sam had changed all that. But Robert didn't know about Sam and his weekly letters. Whatever foolishness had started our letter writing had gotten more serious and tenderer. I might have been a lucky rabbit's foot or a just piece of home in the beginning, but no more.

"Do you know where you're going yet?"

He nodded and fished out a folded and worn envelope from his suit pocket. He held it up, but didn't offer it to me to read. "I'll be working in the state mental hospital in Marlboro, New Jersey."

"Really?" I lowered my voice and scrunched up my nose. It seemed as dangerous as Italy at the moment, but that wasn't something to say out loud. If you were a boy going off to get shot at, you didn't need someone who was going to go live with crazy people making it sound like it was the same sacrifice. "Seems like there'd be easier places to go."

Robert nodded his head. "Probably. But if this war ever ends, I don't want to say I spent it picking asparagus."

"Well," I looked around to make sure no one was in earshot, "I know if I got drafted, I'd put down picking for truck farms as my first choice." I giggled a little. But he looked surprised.

"You? You of all people would be doing something dangerous and noble, like volunteering for medical or starvation experiments. I don't know any girl who's braver than you."

"Me?" I thought through that bit of flattery for a minute but for the life of me couldn't think of any reason why he'd call me brave. Or noble.

"You. Look at how much you helped Suzanne."

Suzanne. The friend as surely lost behind enemy lines as Ben.

"Whatever I did for her didn't do her much good." She'd written once since she'd moved to Wichita. The paper had smelled of something foreign and dangerous—maybe cigarette smoke? And nothing in the letter could be repeated to Mama. I would have rather she'd have played Ben's game and pretended that she was the same girl doing the same things as the one I knew years ago.

"You think every seed you plant is a bean seed? Up five days after you plant it and ready to eat in two months? Suzanne is a walnut tree."

"More like a hedge tree. She's growing some nasty thorns."

Robert cocked his head to the side a bit and smiled. "Maybe. Either way, she needs tending even if you're not seeing anything pretty out of her now."

"I sometimes wonder what I saved her from. She's terribly unhappy now." It surprised me that that popped out of my mouth. She'd never said such a thing, but her letter had cut a wide swath of depression through me, with all its talk about meeting soldier boys from McConnell Air Force Base and going to movies and bobby-pinning up her hair under a bandana every morning to go rivet wings at the Boeing airplane factory.

"How much unhappier would she be if you hadn't come to her rescue?"

I shook my head and tried to picture where she'd be right now. Leavenworth, maybe? I didn't know if she knew how unhappy she was. In that sense, maybe I *had* rescued her. "There's so much more now that I can't save her from."

CHAPTER 13

MAMA AND I WORKED IN the garden. I weeded, she watered and tended. High school was officially over for me. In another era, some good Mennonite boy would be courting me, and I'd be frantically filling my hope chest with embroidered pillowcases and tablecloths and sweet baby things. But this decade was different from all the others anyone living knew, even the ones who'd lived through World War I.

I was impatient. The seed Sam had planted had firmly taken root. Mama, who had her own semester away at college, would surely understand.

"Mama?"

"Hmmm?"

"I'm thinking about going to college in the fall." It was safest to bring this up in the garden. I remembered Ben and the man from Kansas State University and his sadly slanting eyebrows.

"Bible college?"

"Well, it could be Bible college at Hesston." My heart sank a little. I felt itchy to leave the Mennonite womb.

"What would you study? Nursing? Or would you train to be a teacher?"

"I think something more general."

She'd studied Latin herself, so she understood the value of useless knowledge. She didn't say anything.

"I was thinking maybe something like English or history."

"To teach it?"

"I could teach it. Maybe."

"What would you do with that except teach?"

I took a deep breath. "Maybe go into law?"

"Law?" She laughed and stood up from the petunias. If I'd said I wanted to go be a Rockette dancer in New York City, it would have been the very same reaction. "Mercy, girl, where'd you get that outlandish idea—" She stopped, suddenly understanding all the things besides romance that should have made her nervous about those weeks driving around with Sam James. "What would you do with a law degree?"

"Be a lawyer?" I laughed nervously.

Mama just stood there. She was thinking about it, I could tell. But given that in that single sentence I'd fractured every mold made for Mennonite girls, she would have to do a lot of thinking before she could talk. At least the first words out of her mouth hadn't been, "Absolutely not."

Finally she said, "You'd start with English or history? That's what you'd study first?"

"Or political science."

"And if you changed your mind, you could still teach English." It was a statement, not a question, because with the war on and the teacher shortage, if I'd wanted to, I could go back to Sweethome High School as a teacher in the fall. I only needed courage, not a degree.

I nodded.

She pampered the petunias some more. I wanted to talk, even if I just repeated myself, but I counted to ten and then to fifty and then one hundred.

Finally she asked, "How would we pay for it?"

"I could hire myself out. Or maybe get a job in town and stay with the Benders during the week."

She pursed her lips but kept on cultivating the dark dirt around the lively colors.

I'd picked a good moment to talk about this. I could feel it.

She did a thinking-kind of a sigh and said, "I doubt that'd be enough money. Not for tuition and room and board."

"Maybe I could get a part-time job while I'm in school." I felt more hope than was safe. It was all I could do not to rush the conversation.

She nodded in a distracted sort of way but didn't say anything. In fact, that was pretty much the end of the exchange. As much as I wanted a yes or no, I just kept weeding. The one strategy that never worked with Mama was badgering. She always said that not talking built more character than talking and even if her children didn't have anything but character, at least they'd have that. Or at least I'd have it. It was going on four months since Ben had been captured. He'd drifted out of our constant conversation. He'd never left our thoughts for an hour, though.

It started to pick up and blow like it was fixing to storm but good. The cottonwoods swished their branches and rattled their leaves. I left Mama to finish in the garden and went inside and started dinner. By the time we sat down to eat, the rain sounded like pebbles against the windows.

"LeRoy Fitch drove by while I was out on the south forty," Dad said and sopped up some gravy with his biscuit. He hardly ever initiated talk at meals. "Those are the folks that bought the old Hallsey place." The Dalkees, Bowens, and Kistlers had all lived on that farm after the Hallseys did, but how would anyone know what place we were talking about if we kept calling it something else? "They got two sets of twin boys that aren't even in school yet, a little fella that might be in first or second grade, and another one on the way real soon." Dad pointed his chin at me while he took care of the last drop of gravy. "LeRoy wondered if maybe they could hire you to come help the missus. At least till the baby came, maybe longer."

Providence. Who would have thought? Maybe there was something to this prayer business after all.

I looked at Mama. She looked at me and lifted her eyebrows. She must have also seen providence in the moment.

"I could do that." Shoot, I could herd chickens if I thought it would put money toward college. Come to think of it, I probably would have preferred chickens to five little boys.

"How much are they willing to pay?" Mama asked.

Dad looked surprised, but he had an answer. "Ten dollars a week."

Mama looked at me again. "That's pretty good. You could make more in Sweethome, but we'd have to pay Edwin and Tilly something for your keep. And you'd be gone all week. This way you could come home every night and still help out some here."

Dad's one eyebrow lifted up. Not that he would've opposed all the money talk, but this wasn't the conversation he thought we'd be having, I'm sure. But since he started conversations so rarely, he also didn't know how to control them when they got out of hand.

"If they took you through the end of August, that'd be almost a hundred and twenty dollars." Mama nodded.

Dad smiled a half smile. "That'd be right nice to have that extra money. The wheat's been good, but with that we could buy ourselves a newer truck."

"Or pay for a semester of college for Cat."

Dad's face flushed. "What? Why would— We can't afford—"

"Ezra," Mama said about as firmly as I'd ever heard her talk. "This'll be a whole lot cheaper than a basketball scholarship to Kansas State University."

Nope. This was definitely not the conversation he thought he'd started.

The following Monday morning I saddled Little Willy and headed across our section, cutting through the pasture and fallow fields, skirting the silky acres of yellowing wheat. Well before I reached the road, I came to the knoll just above the Schmidt place. Little Willy paused only a moment before he nosed down toward the barnyard. I jerked on the reins, too harshly I know. Poor Little Willy didn't know we weren't headed there. This had been our destination a thousand times except for the last three years when we'd traveled here together only twice. Yet he was going home as surely as his own barn.

Little Willy didn't understand and insisted on plodding down the hill toward the barn and mulberry tree. I reined him back. Old and tired like he was, he still snorted impatiently.

"Just wait, Little Willy," I said to him softly and stroked his neck. Being in this spot and seeing the dusty, ragged farmstead below again made my stomach churn. What if that hot July day I'd left home fifteen minutes earlier? What if I'd arrived just in time to catch Suzanne as she flew out of her house to the barn? What if I'd swept her up and we'd ridden over the cinnamon hills to Oklahoma—away from Simon Yoder, away from Marie and Henry?

I tried to picture the chain of events and suddenly felt guilty because I realized I never would have met Sam.

It wouldn't have worked, though. She couldn't have stayed lost. They would have found her and brought her back to Simon's. Like they'd done with Dess. Her fate would have been the same. Maybe worse, although I couldn't quite grasp what that would be. Jail *was* better. Suzanne had said it herself over and over. I believed her then and now. A piece I never thought about much anymore was that there weren't any more girls after Suzanne. She was the final one. How many girls had she saved by sacrificing herself?

Little Willy whinnied softly. I wanted to leave, too, but at that moment the haymow doors opened and I saw a man—Henry Schmidt, I'm sure, not a ghost—standing at the edge. His arms reached up to the cross brace above him. He leaned out over the ground like he was studying it.

I didn't know until that moment that he also struggled with turning the clock back. But what other meaning could I take from seeing him there?

The painful memories compressed my chest. I was afraid I'd stop breathing. I nudged Little Willy to turn and head for the Hallsey place. He snorted, annoyed that he wouldn't be nibbling on mulberry-sweetened grass all day. As I reined Little Willy to point north, Henry's head turned toward us. We both froze. He'd seen me three years ago, almost to the day, in this very spot.

Dad always said that if you always got what you wanted, you'd never choose life's hardest experiences. Yet some of the very best parts of life came out of those times.

Sam or no Sam, I don't think either Henry or I would agree with that this morning.

CHAPTER 14

THE RED-JAM HANDPRINT ON THE kitchen door window should have been a warning. It started about halfway down the pane—far higher than the body for that miniature signature could ever reach—and slid down to where it disappeared into the wood, for all the world looking like some kind of a nursery school SOS.

I knocked anyway.

Shrill, birdlike voices gathered on the other side. I could see their heads bobbing, all five of them. The biggest one ordered the others to stand back and yanked the door open.

"Good morning," I said, and smiled like I planned to be in control.

They just stared at me. If they'd used a cookie cutter to make these boys, they couldn't have made them more alike: all of them with soft, sand-colored curls, round blue eyes, and half smiles pulled up to the left. All five wore overalls that looked like any one of them could have been part of the jam adventure.

"Is your daddy or mama here?"

They all still stared, but the biggest one kind of nodded. One of the littlest ones finally turned around, ran to the parlor, and pointed to an unseen part of the room. "She's in here," he said poking with every word, "and she cain't move!"

The others opened a pathway for me and I raced into the front room, expecting to see Mrs. Fitch hurt, unable to get up. Instead, a worn-looking woman lay on the couch, with those same round blue eyes and half-tilted smile—all considerably more weary than the boys'—and looking for all the world like she was hiding a huge watermelon under her housedress.

"Bedrest. The doctor ordered it, and the boys cain't understand it 'cause that's the last place they'd ever plant their fannies on a summer day," she said and extended a hand for me to shake. "You must be Cat."

"And you look like the only one here who could be Mrs. Fitch." It was a goofy thing to say, but we both laughed.

"That I am. But call me Martha." She had a twangy Oklahoma drawl and a sweet, easy grin, the kind that makes you like a body right from the start without knowing the first thing about her. "Boys, this is Cat Peters. She's the one who's here to help us until the baby comes. Cat, this is Earl, Robert, Richard, Jimmy and Johnny."

Jimmy or Johnny, the one who had pointed into the parlor, burst into tears and threw himself on his mother's shoulder. "You said *a cat* was coming over to take care of us, not a girl!"

Martha immediately wrapped soothing arms around the boy and oozed, "Oh, Buddyboy, I'm sorry she ain't a real cat." But she grew tiny tears in the corner of her eyes and her giant belly shook from smothered laughs.

"RrrrrMeeowww!" I did my best snarling cat imitation, pulled out of some childhood memory and years of barnyard cat encounters.

Jimmy or Johnny gave me a horrified one-eyed peek and then buried his face in his mama's shoulder again. The other twin, in contrast, squealed, "Do it again!"

So I did.

"Again!"

Martha gave me a sympathetic look. But she was the one pregnant with her sixth child.

"RrrrrMeeowwwletsgo."

All five Fitch boys stared at me. I'd captured their attention, but didn't have a clue what I was going to do with it. And I certainly wasn't going to talk cat-talk till September. Nevertheless, I slunk, feline-like, back through the kitchen and summer porch and on out by the washhouse. I was a magnet. All five boys not only followed me, but they, too, began to slide their arms and shoulders and legs as though they were my kittens.

"Meeoowww," I said to them. It was a good thing I was going off to college. I'd make a ludicrous mother if this was the best I could do.

"Meow, meow, meow," they purred back.

I found a washtub and filled it with water for them to play in—and get even dirtier—while I started heating the wash water. It was a Monday, the universal washday. I didn't even have to ask Martha what to do first.

While they were momentarily distracted, I went back into the house and gathered the laundry and wiped off the jungle of jam prints in the tiny but otherwise tidy kitchen. I'd been there less than a half hour and already felt completely overwhelmed about managing five boys and a household for a day, let alone a week or a month or more. But Martha said the right thing to me: "Youall's an angel sent from God, ain't ya? Youall've just given me more peace and quiet in the last fifteen minutes than I had since the last twins was born." As the folks from Oklahoma do, she turned every syllable into two, and every two into three.

By the time I got back to the washhouse, the boys, except for Earl, were all naked as a bunch of jaybirds. They splashed in and out of the tub, carrying mason jars of water to a corner of the yard where they decided they were going to build a fishing pond so they wouldn't have to walk clear out to the pasture.

We muddled—or should I say muddied—through the morning like this. I struggled with the laundry while they turned the dirt in front of the washhouse into a bog. At dinner, I apologized to Martha and her husband, LeRoy— who looked every inch as tired as Martha—about how we'd destroyed the yard. But Martha just weakly waved her hand and said, "Did they kill any animals or start any fires or run any cars off the road?"

I shook my head and laughed.

"Then your week's already goin' better than mine did last week."

I laughed nervously because she said, "It ain't a joke, Cat. Youall's gonna earn your money." And then she made some vague reference to a squirrel that was in the wrong place at the wrong time.

So that was how I measured my days with the Fitch boys: if nothing died, nothing burned, and no cars landed in the ditch out front, it was a good day. Not every day was a good day, and I can tell you for a fact that it was an especially good thing no more than two or three cars drove past the Fitch place on any one day.

Fortunately, none of the boys had a mean bone in him. I know Mrs. Alvin P. Pendermaust might argue with me, since she just happened to drive past the very same moment the amphibian and reptile experiment peaked. But it wasn't like the boys had *planned* to scare her into apoplexy by dropping a bushel of frogs and garter snakes out of the trees one by one to see if—given enough chances—they could fly. Poor Mrs. Pendermaust thought for sure the good Lord was visiting another plague on the world just like he did on the Egyptians in Bible times.

I know all this sounds like cruelty to animals, but the Fitch boys were more in the camp of loving animals so much that they hugged them to death—I say this in spite of the amphibian and reptile experiment and the subsequent chicken incident, pig rodeo, and that truly most unfortunate baby rabbit fiasco. Each time, they were just trying to expand the poor animal's horizons, as well as their own. Either Jimmy or Johnny told me in all seriousness that when he grew up he wanted to be a marmot.

Personally, I would have liked to have been in better control, but it wasn't going to happen, so I did my best to prevent death, destruction, and fire; keep the kitchen clean; put food on the table at meals; and finish enough laundry that the boys didn't have to play naked except on wash days.

And some days I did.

CHAPTER 15

HENRY SCHMIDT WAS LIKE SANDPAPER in my shoe.

Every morning Little Willy and I followed the patchwork quilt of fields and pastures until we came to the knoll above the Schmidt farm. From there, we turned north to the Fitches. Nearly every morning, Little Willy paused, as though he couldn't believe we weren't headed down to the sticky sweet mulberry grass at the edge of the Schmidt barnyard. Most mornings Henry stood in the door of the haymow. We were a ritual now. Neither of us ever waved.

Early evening as Little Willy and I plodded back home, we would once again pass the shabby place. Little Willy never paused or headed down the knoll. This time of the day as the colors gathered bouquet like in the sky, all he wanted was his own stall and fresh hay.

I hardly ever saw Henry in the evenings, but sometimes heard the milk canisters faintly clanging behind the faded and peeling walls of the barn. After the frenzied days with the Fitch boys, the emptiness and disorder of the Schmidt farmyard overwhelmed me, leaving me unsettled, depressed.

I could have taken a few extra minutes and made the trip by the road, avoiding the place altogether, but I didn't. I dreaded—yet was drawn—to the knoll.

Henry and I never acknowledged each other on Sundays, either. I usually sat at least a few rows behind him. I watched his thick, leathery red neck, trying my best to pierce inside to see what he must be thinking. He never gave up his secrets. He sang, knelt and prayed, and occasionally snored like all the other men on that side of the aisle. No one would chide him on the way home for the snores. It was a lonely thought.

By the middle of July, Martha Fitch looked ready to burst at the seams. That baby—and we were all praying it was going to be *a* baby, not babies—would arrive any day if the doctor was right. I just wanted it to come during the night and not on a washday. What if the doctor showed up and the Fitch boys were all naked and playing with a tub full of captured critters?

I'd go to jail.

I think Martha, on the other hand, prayed fervently that the baby would come when the most hands were available. God could have construed this to mean harvest time but thankfully knew better than to add a delivery and newborn to that chaos. Those days of waiting I did my best to keep the boys outside but within earshot of any noise that might signal the onset of labor. The boys had taken to playing Allies and Axis in the European theater, usually with an incongruous assortment of imaginary animals—horses, dogs, and cats, of course, but also bears, deer, wolves, squirrels, and the occasional marmot. It was more like cowboys against Indians at a zoo governed by Hitler.

I was very tired of the wars, both the real one and the imaginary one. The week the baby came, I had finally convinced the boys to be pioneers in covered wagons. They spent hours every morning packing their wagon with food, water, and supplies, and more hours deciding what route to take, who got to be the attacking animals, and when and how the surprise skirmishes should take place. It disappointed them that the Indians were only friendly, but I told them there was enough real dying in the world going on. They didn't need to add any pretend dying and that included animals.

I think the thing that finally sent Martha into labor was that on Thursday the boys decided they'd been pioneers long enough, so I let them go down to the creek to pan for gold. The water was low and slow enough that in order to drown, they'd have to fall asleep face down in the muddy water, which was highly unlikely. I stayed back at the house to do some mending and get dinner on. Martha lay on the davenport, restless and puffy looking. Sometimes when I stayed in the house, we talked. I more or less untangled the stories about Sam, Ben, Suzanne, and even my hopes for college and dreams of becoming an attorney. My Simon, Ethel, and Henry stories were more knots than tangles, but I tried to explain them, too. I probably shouldn't have talked about them since that bordered on the vilest kind of gossip—except that gossip isn't true and everything I said was. Besides, I just kind of fell into it the first time I talked about Sam. How else do you explain a Mennonite girl and a Methodist attorney? Left unsaid was my hope for a James & James future.

Martha reciprocated. I knew about her courtship with LeRoy, the modest wealth she'd grown up with, her childless sister in Oklahoma who wanted nothing more than her own passel of kids but had a passel of cats instead, and the heartache of her sister who'd run away with a colored man and now had four nut-brown babies of their own. This sister lived on the edges of the white folks' and the colored folks' world in the Kansas City jungle, accepted by neither, distrusted by both. Yet she said she was happy. Martha thought her nut-brown babies might say otherwise.

I liked Martha. LeRoy, too. And even though I left exhausted every evening, it was a good exhaustion, not like the fearful weeks I'd spent as the hired girl for Simon and Ethel.

That Thursday, though, Martha just tried to stay quiet, as though she knew she had to be storing every second of peace. She asked if I would sing to her, which I did, mostly hymns we both knew, but also some radio songs like "As Time Goes By" and "You'd Be So Nice to Come Home To." I couldn't sing like Dinah Shore, but Martha and I still both cried, so I went back to hymns while I rolled out the biscuits and made gravy for the potatoes.

Just before noon the boys came back, excited as a beehive about all the gold they'd found. They scrubbed their hands and faces. I'd be mopping the floor that afternoon. I noticed as they washed up they looked kind of bulgy.

"You got something in those pockets, boys?"

"Yup!" a couple of them said proudly.

"We got gold!"

I'd helped Martha up and she stood and stretched at the table a moment while LeRoy washed up. She kissed the tops of several curly heads.

"What kinda gold you boys find?" Martha asked.

"The best kind!" Their eyes shone.

"Well, sit down so we can eat."

"Cain't."

"Cain't what?"

"Cain't sit down."

"Why not?"

"We'll squish the gold."

Martha and I looked at each other.

LeRoy scratched his cheek. "Well, boys, you'll just have to empty the gold so yo'all can si'down."

The boys looked sadly at each other, but Johnny obediently reached into a pocket and pulled out a frog. He dropped it on the floor and reached into the pocket for another one. The first frog, thrilled to be free of its denim prison, sprang toward the parlor.

I shrieked, I know I did.

By the time the second frog hit the linoleum, the frogs in the other boys' pockets—driven by some primal understanding that their kin were escaping—began scrambling upward and outward. Frogs struggled out of pockets and gaps between overalls and skin. Frog after frog leaped across the floor and chairs and table.

Only Earl hung on to his gold, but I don't know why or how.

When every pocket looked empty, Jimmy and Johnny stuck their pudgy hands inside their overalls into, I guess, their undershorts and methodically started removing the gold they'd carried there.

I didn't know there were that many frogs in all of Kiowa County. How those boys could have walked all the way up from the creek with those things clambering for fresh air against all that little boy skin, I'll never know.

I have to admit I kept on shrieking. The frogs were everywhere and going more places. Martha was laughing so hard that none of us noticed at first that a puddle of water had formed under her until Earl, who'd still managed to contain his colony of frogs up until that moment, pointed at the puddle and announced, horrified, "Mama's peed her pants."

Now the boys started squealing along with me, half laughing, half crying that their Mama could cross this line in nature.

Martha's eyes grew big. "It ain't pee," she gasped and clutched her abdomen. "Call the doc," she wheezed. "Call your mama." She nodded at me.

It was quite the sight seeing the frogs flying around the room, hugely pregnant Martha leaning on LeRoy's arm as she hobbled up the stairs, and those five, curly-haired Fitch boys frantically chasing their gold.

I rang Mable Higbee, the town operator, and told her to get Doc Sipple and my mama out to the old Hallsey place fast. If I'd told her to send him to the Fitch place, the doc would have wondered around the countryside long enough for that baby to be born and start teething before he would've found us.

I gathered the clean rags we'd set aside and started boiling water, then set to clearing the frogs out of the house before Mama could get there and wonder what in the world the Fitches had been paying me for.

Mama got there in time to set LeRoy on a chair to keep him from passing out and catch sweet little Amy Marcella Fitch. By the time the doc arrived, there wasn't much left for him to do except clean up the mess and take credit for another successful delivery. By then, most of the frogs were leaping toward the creek again, except for the one that now lived somewhere in a kitchen cupboard and croaked every so often to remind us that in the eternal struggle of man against nature, for the time being, nature was still winning.

Amy was Amy only long enough to lay claim to the name. Before Doc Sipple left, she was already Sweetpea. With all those brothers, even joyful but buzzing with energy like they were, she probably needed a name like Chimera—that fire-breathing female monster with a lion's head, a goat's body, and a serpent's tail from Greek mythology—to hold her own. If fact, that might not have been such a bad plan since that would have made her part animal.

I stayed over the first few nights until Martha's mama, Mrs. Gertie Baumgartner, could come up from Pawhuska, Oklahoma, and be there around the clock. Martha's mama seemed like a nice enough lady, but within a few hours, I realized that for the next two weeks, I'd be taking care of all five Fitch boys, Martha, LeRoy, and Mrs. Baumgartner, who had never washed a dish in her life. Mrs. Baumgartner mostly needed to lie down and rest and didn't want any boy noise in the house. Of course, the boys only wanted to be *in* the house since that's where Sweetpea was. And they certainly couldn't help it that where their feet were, their mouths were too, and it all kept moving. We finally compromised and they spent a lot of those first days taking turns sitting in the tree outside their mama's window and shushing each other. The only one I really wanted to take care of was Sweetpea, but the line was too long, so I just kept cooking, cleaning, wiping noses, washing and hanging laundry, dusting, sweeping, corralling boys, and thanking the good Lord I was headed for a college education so I'd have a little more time before I started having babies of my own to take care of.

Even though those Fitch boys made me laugh every day, Little Willy and I dragged home every night, both of us feeling overworked and underpaid. Early August we were plodding along one evening, achy and tired and feeling ever so sorry for myself because woman-of-leisure Gertie Baumgartner—who couldn't get her own glass of water—was requiring more work than Martha and Sweetpea combined.

Kansas is always more sky than land anyway, but that evening the colors drenched us in firecracker reds and oranges. The sun, a blazing fist, sank onto the horizon just as we reached the knoll above the Schmidt farm. I stopped Little Willy and watched the world for several minutes as the colors melted and dusk draped the land. Below us, the Schmidt farm was soundless except for animals rustling and the soft swish of the cottonwoods. Only the kitchen light was on, a single yellow dot in the midst of rapidly lengthening blue shadows. I'd be home with Dad and Mama in a few minutes. They'd have already eaten supper and might even be reading in bed, but there would be warm bodies in my house. If I wanted to talk, it wouldn't be to myself.

Once upon a time, the Schmidts had been as loud and happy as the Fitches. And now it was just Henry, who was sad and empty of everything.

Little Willy snorted and whinnied a little, eager to be home, so we turned and picked our way across the wheat stubble. Henry had chosen his path and there wasn't anything anyone could do to change it.

CHAPTER 16

Blame it on Westinghouse. Or I suppose you could blame it on Mrs. Gertie-I-cain't-lift-a-finger Baumgartner who couldn't change a diaper but could at least write a check (which also explained how it came to be that LeRoy and Martha could afford having a hired girl). The folks from Razook Appliance store in Greensburg delivered a deluxe new stove with push-button temperature controls the week she left to go back to Pawhuska. If you set the oven control to three hundred and fifty degrees, in minutes, it climbed to and stayed at three hundred and fifty degrees. What a magical thing!

Anyway, that and Mrs. Baumgartner's other gift of an envelope of black-market sugar coupons sent me into a baking frenzy. Cookies, pies, cakes, cinnamon rolls, fancy breads—I'd never turned out anything so repeatedly perfect. The best part was that the boys had been so sugar-deprived since rationing began that even though I still used the wartime recipes that had about as much sugar as a lemon, a cookie was a cookie. Those boys had no shame, no shame at all in how easily they could be bribed. They were better, cleaner, harder working, and I think even smarter those last two weeks before I went off to college.

Most nights, Martha insisted I take some of the extra baked goods home to Dad and Mama. This created an awkward discussion at my house, but only the first evening. Black market coupons were illegal. No matter how much we longed for things, and—ironically—how much extra money we had those days to buy the coupons, Dad wouldn't cross that line. Barter, yes. Buy, no. Cookies made from black market sugar seemed to fall irrationally into the buy column, not the barter one.

Mama and I were more pragmatic. We celebrated with a cup each of real coffee that first night and let those cookies melt on our tongues. Dad thought we were wasting good coffee on a little sin.

Finally, I convinced him to join us. "I think I made these cookies with what was left in the sugar canister. This wasn't the black market bag."

Dad's eye twitched briefly, but his shoulders relaxed a little. In the end, he smiled, winked, and helped himself. "Then we'll just have to pray for a never-ending canister of old sugar, just like Elisha and the bottomless jug of oil and flour."

My last day at the Fitches', the clouds dropped to the ground. It didn't so much rain as it just shrouded the world in a dewy freshness. Martha let me hold Sweetpea all afternoon while she baked up her special Dutch apple pie, with its crunchy sweet top, to send home with me. The real recipe called for a whole cup of sugar and she used every grain. Sweetpea practiced stretching and squeaking and stealing my heart, which didn't take any true practice on her part at all. Martha and I talked sister talk because that's what both of us had finally decided we were. She would miss me. I would miss her. I would miss the boys. I wouldn't miss the frogs.

When I left, each of the boys kissed me and promised to be good. I left feeling teary but nourished.

Little Willy and I headed south, across the damp furrowed fields, our precious apple pie carefully packed for the ride. The weather had cleared out, leaving that fresh, earthy scent that this evening mingled with the perfume of apples and sugar-crunch topping. Sunflowers lined the culverts, their heads all bent in benediction toward the setting sun. Crows cawed from the hedgerow, singing to the evening and the distraction of a horse and a girl and a sweet-smelling pie tramping through their world.

A few clouds still hung on the horizon, blocking the sun until its last moment on earth when it found a slit in the pack and shot rays of hot, yellow light across the hills. It was a hymn to the evening, not the mellow, quiet kind, but a roaring hallelujah of beauty. By the time Little Willy and I reached the knoll above the Schmidts, the evening had dissolved into gray. Once again, only a single light burned in the kitchen. It couldn't pierce the darkness, though, because the vast emptiness swallowed it up.

I paused there, maybe a moment too long, breathing in the scent of the slightly warm pie and the earth and feeling the sadness that seemed to creep through the barnyard below and flow, river like, up the knoll and across the land. Almost without thinking, I pointed Little Willy down to the light. Little Willy at first whinnied in protest. He was old and tired and just wanted to be home. But he was also so old and tired he didn't have much protest left in him, so he plodded down to his spot by the mulberry tree. At least one of us would eat something sweet tonight.

I crept through the ghosts in the farmyard—the Cyclops eye of the haymow, the lifeless patch where the garden used to be, the empty summer porch where Suzanne and I dragged a mattress out to sleep on those hot, still summer nights. Like a tattered shawl, the evening shadows draped the scattered farm implements and broken fences, hiding the decay but never taking it away. Animals rustled and grunted behind the barn doors.

Before I reached the house, Henry must have heard me. He came out onto the summer porch and opened the screen door. A diluted wedge of light fell around him, leaving his face in the dark.

"Someone there?" His voice sounded thick and rough. In a week, how many words would he use?

"It's me. Cat." I reached the light of the open door.

"Cat?" He hadn't washed his hair or shaved since probably Sunday. Gray stubble marked the heaviness in his face. "Is something wrong?"

I took a deep breath. I don't know what had possessed me to do this, but now I couldn't turn and leave without finishing. I shook my head. "Everything is fine." My hands shook slightly. "I brought you an apple pie."

"A pie? For me?" Emotion thickened his voice more. "Whatever for?" I could hear the disbelief in his words.

Whatever for? I didn't know myself. I just vaguely shrugged my shoulders.

"Come in, come in." He opened the door wider, and his voice might have brightened a bit. "I was just fixin' to eat a little supper." I stepped in the house, then immediately regretted it. Beside the jumbled mess of the table behind him was a chipped green plate, the kind we all got out of cereal boxes in the Depression. It looked like supper was a couple of fried eggs and a chunk of bread. The sink and small workspace were stacked with dirty dishes and pans, as though one dish got washed at a time—the one he planned to eat off of. Even if the farmyard had never been a neat place, Marie and the girls had always kept a clean kitchen, or at least as clean as a body could keep a space that invited blowing dust in through a dozen cracks. The mess made me dizzy.

In the light of the kitchen, I could see that Henry's eyes were red and watery.

"I really shouldn't stay. Dad and Mama'll wonder what's taking me so long."

He nodded. "Surely. I understand." He looked at the wall behind me. "I just don't get many visitors these days, so you're a real bright spot."

I handed him the pie. Our fingers collided as he took the pie from me. Who would have touched him in the last six months? Did anyone ever even shake his hand on a Sunday? How much would a soul shrivel without words or human contact?

"Are you sure you won't stay and eat a slice with me?"

I wanted to leave. Ached to be home. But it wasn't the pie he needed, I finally realized. So I sat at the kitchen table and cleared a spot while he put on water for coffee and washed another dish. I wondered if he regretted the awkwardness of the moment, but I don't think so. I fumbled for small talk, anything to put some sound in the room.

"I'm going off to Hesston College next week." The Mennonite womb was as familiar to him as the chipped dinner plate.

"That so? That's real good." He took out real coffee, not Postum, and measured a couple of tablespoons into the filter. "You're a smart girl. You'll do real good there."

He put a kind of clean plate, fork, and cup in front of me. And then he did an odd but touching thing: he found a clean cloth napkin and put it beside my plate. It probably hadn't been used since Marie had last invited company. How many years ago was that?

"Do you hear anything about Ben?" He asked it so kindly I was afraid I'd cry.

I shook my head.

His voice filled with that earlier huskiness. "It's hard, ain't it? Not knowing."

"It is." My own voice was husky now.

The coffee perked too slowly.

"There's a lot of things a body'd do different if they just had the chance."

I didn't know if he meant Ben, or Dad and Mama, or me, or Suzanne. Maybe he was talking about himself.

We fell quiet. Henry wasn't very practiced at making conversation these days, and I was filled with too many things to say that couldn't be said, so I just sat there.

Eventually, he poured the coffee and sliced the pie into World War II pieces, the kind that were thin enough to see through. My insides finally settled enough, and I started talking about the Fitch family a little and baby Sweetpea and how those boys were a handful, but they surely loved frogs. He chuckled a little and told me a story about when Inez and Anna Joy were just little squirts, they kept a frog family for a few weeks and even badgered Marie into making some frog clothes. He had tiny tears at the corner of his eyes as he told the story.

I finished my coffee and said I had to get going. Henry wouldn't let me leave without cutting off a nice hunk of the pie for Dad and Mama. It was a kind thing to do.

Little Willy and I headed home then into the face of the rising moon. The yellow dot of light at the Schmidt place stayed on until we were over the knoll.

I didn't know why my heart ached so. I also didn't know why of all moments I thought of Ethel then. I thought I'd gotten rid of her years ago.

CHAPTER 17

IT TURNED OUT THAT IN 1943 Hesston College was a convent: one hundred fifteen girls and six boys. I don't know what I was thinking, or if it would have even made any difference if I'd thought through the numbers, but it still surprised me. It didn't matter that every boy I knew was either in the military, in Civilian Public Service, or a 4F. It still hadn't registered that the only boys I'd be in school with would either be old, infirm, or married. And I wasn't even looking. I felt sorry for the other hundred and fourteen girls who might have been in the marrying mood. They were plumb and peach out of luck.

I had a nice enough roommate, Pearl Shenk from Cheraw, Colorado, but she could be too loud and bossy. Her dad directed the tuberculosis sanitarium that the Mennonites ran in Cheraw. She knew my cousins, the Headrick girls, there in Cheraw, but she only announced that they were loud and bossy. I already knew that, and I told her there must be something in the water at Cheraw. It took her a minute, but then she started to laugh, so I knew we could be friends after that. Poor Pearl was unbearably homesick. I guess my second semester of my senior year I'd faced that demon. Surely, I missed Mama, but tears only made everyone else miserable. They didn't take me home. Pearl thought her family lived on the other side of the world, even though they only lived another two hundred miles west from Sweethome. There were girls at school from Pennsylvania and Virginia, even New York. Now *that* was far enough away to make the spirit burst. I told Pearl that your family lives in your heart, and if they were truly there, it didn't matter whether you were five miles or five thousand miles away. And if you didn't have them in your heart, you could be lonely in the same room as they were. For years after we left Hesston, she'd write in her Christmas letter how much she appreciated that bit of wisdom.

Fortunately, that first semester I got lots of letters. Mama, and even Dad, wrote at least once a week. Sam, with his exotic cryptic military return address, wrote his regular weekly epistle, and even Robert Miller corresponded every now and then. I didn't ever talk about Ben, but since this was a Mennonite college and nearly everyone was connected by invisible string to someone else, the word got out soon enough. Pearl was sufficiently in awe of this unspeakable situation that she ordered everyone else to stop asking me about it. This is an example of when it's good to have a loud, bossy friend. I was exotic to her. I couldn't imagine this even though the most foreign thing Pearl had done so far in her life was a blind date with a Mexican boy to the Colorado

State fair, which, of course, she talked about incessantly. And loudly.

The other letter I got early on was postmarked Sweethome. There wasn't any return address and the jerky scrawl was unfamiliar. It turned out to be from Henry:

Dear Cat,

Thank you for the apple pie. It was the kindest thing anyone has done for me since Marie passed away. It has been very lonely here.

The maize is looking real good. I hope it will be a good crop this year. I hope your enjoying school.
Sincerely,
Henry Schmidt

I folded the letter back up and stuck it into my American literature book and then for some reason carried it around for weeks. When the book fell open to that page, I'd read those simple lines again. Henry wasn't like Ethel was for me. He destroyed his own children, and so by friendship, I was pulled into that murkiness, but I personally never felt his bite. Maybe this is why his loneliness nagged at me like it did.

His empty mailbox slipped into my thoughts. Finally, I sent a short note back to him. His thank you didn't require it, but if I ever thought it was important to give something to someone, this was it. I told him how my classes were going and that I was making a lot of new friends. Safe things to say. But they were words for him to read and carry in his pocket.

They were something human to bear him from Sunday to Sunday.

He wrote back. Oddly enough, it came in the same mail as a letter from Suzanne. I didn't want a correspondence with Henry. I just wanted to lift his spirits. He wrote about the maize crop again and about stopping by the old Hallsey place to return the pie plate to Martha Fitch. He reported that Sweetpea surely was a sweet thing and those boys were full of spunk. It worried me that, thanks to my gossip, Martha knew more about Henry than Henry knew about Martha. I just had to trust that she'd be discreet, and I thanked the good Lord she hadn't been drinking Cheraw water for what she might say to him.

Suzanne, in contrast, simply wrote she was coming to Hesston for the weekend. She didn't ask, she just announced it to me. Wichita was only an hour's bus ride away. She would come on Saturday and leave on Sunday and sleep on the floor in my room. I got the letter on Wednesday of that week, so even if I didn't like the plan, short of a telegram or a phone call—both mostly reserved for deaths and births—I had no way of reaching her.

I'm not entirely sure why I didn't want her to come, except that our worlds orbited different suns these days. I didn't know if I could explain her to Pearl or to any of my other friends. Even if Suzanne and I never said a word about her past to anyone, by the end of the weekend, everyone would know she was *that* Suzanne Schmidt. Those invisible strings pulled in every direction. Pearl, on the other hand, would make lots of sense to Suzanne. Once a Mennonite, always a Mennonite. No matter how hard she tried, she'd never be able to shake that dust off.

I had to get permission from Genevieve Kaufman, the dorm matron, which was easy enough to do, but only because she didn't fully understand who was coming. Miss Kaufman told me that as long as Suzanne abided by the rules, including lights out at ten thirty, she couldn't imagine any problems. I could see she had a limited imagination.

That Saturday, the air chilled a body to the bone. It was one of those typical Kansas things. The temperature read sixty, but the wind flew along the streets, blowing leaves and rattling teeth. I sat in the post office and waited for the bus to pull in to town and looked at all the wanted posters while I waited. I didn't recognize anyone, but I memorized faces just in case. A windfall was a windfall.

When Suzanne stepped off the bus, I hardly recognized her. She had that familiar Schmidt body, but her red lips and made-up eyes looked ghost-like. She waved back at a couple of green-clad boys and blew a kiss.

"Hi!" She threw her arms around me and laughed like an escaped schoolgirl. "Isn't this grand? We're only a short bus ride away from each other now." She locked her arm through mine and started to walk in the direction of the college. "I can send you money to come visit me in Wichita, and I'll come see you here."

The leaves scattered furiously in front of us as we walked. Orange, red, bronze, purple. Sunset colors. She talked in empty ways while we headed back to my room—about eyeshadow and movies and running an electric drill. If she'd talked Latin, I would have been able to converse better. I have to say my heart sank. I started to worry that the return bus to Wichita would break down west of town and she'd never be able to leave. All this outside color of hers—the makeup, the chatter—seemed tinny, like a tough veneer hiding a hollow center.

But she was shiny on the outside, so she drew people to her. All afternoon, my friends wandered in and out of my room, hoping to spend a little time in the same space as this foreign girl. Suzanne drew the oddest things out of those girls, getting them to nod and giggle as though they, too, had struggled with caking lipstick and lived with secret crushes on dreamy Tyrone Powers. It's human nature to want to be like everyone else, even if the everyone else is only a single lost girl.

After supper, we walked into the blue evening, out past the edge of campus and along the black furrowed fields of newly planted winter wheat.

Suzanne fidgeted. She kept chattering but changed the subject every other sentence, never mind that each thought was as aimless as the last. When we were well out of sight of tattletale college eyes, she pulled out a package of cigarettes and lit one. If she'd taken off all of her clothes and run naked into the wind, I would have been less startled.

Suzanne blew out a puff of white, curly smoke and rolled her eyes at my expression. "It's not a big deal, Cat. Don't give me those big eyes."

"Smoking. Really."

She slid a shoulder up like she'd done the year in between the death and the sentence. She drew in another breath and let the smoke flow out of her mouth as she talked. "Why not?" She held her arm out at an odd angle. The cigarette rested between two stiff, straight fingers.

I'd never seen a girl smoke. This distracted me, and I didn't talk.

"Any word about Ben?" She asked and blew a cloud of smoke back towards campus.

Any word about Ben. It was a question that was meant to be kind but it wasn't.

"No. No word about Ben." My stomach twisted into a knot. I hadn't talked about him with anyone since I'd left home.

She shook her head and we walked. "Not knowing keeps you awake at night."

Tears brimmed my eyes, but she couldn't see them.

Minutes passed. Then she asked, "Are you happy here?"

I didn't answer immediately, more because I wasn't sure of her tone than because I had to decide on the answer. Besides, I was smelling that cigarette smoke.

Finally I said, "I am. I like my classes. The people are very nice. I've made a lot of friends."

"You don't feel smothered? Claustrophobic?" She blew out a stream of smoke. I could tell in this single cigarette that she loved the drama smoking added to her words. "They tell you how long your skirt has to be, when to eat, when to study, when to turn the lights out at night. For heaven's sake, they lock the door so you can't leave at night or come in late.

You couldn't even drag a mattress out on a summer porch to sleep when it's hot." She snorted and rolled her eyes. "They make you go to chapel every day and church on Sunday. What's left for you to decide? What day to write home? They probably censor your letters, too."

"You make it sound like jail."

"Isn't it?"

"Well, I *chose* to come here." What was I saying?

Suzanne ignored the ugly reminder. She smoked her cigarette some more. In between puffs, her arm stretched out at that odd angle away from her coat.

"Are *you* happy?" I asked. Maybe that was why she asked me.

"Sure." But she said it without conviction. "I have a job. I make lots of money. I make my own decisions." She looked at me grimly. "I'm not in jail."

We hadn't done well with our conversation since she'd stepped off the bus. It was either pointless, empty talk, or this that had sharp edges to it.

Abruptly, she said, "Anna Joy's got a serious beau."

"Will they get married?"

She slid her shoulder up again. I'd forgotten what a statement that made. "Probably. He's in the military and will get shipped out in the next few weeks." Her cigarette was finally done. She dropped it onto the sandy road, a fiery red dot at our feet. She ignored it. "He's a creep. I think she's making a mistake, but she's made so many already." She left the thought hanging. I think she muttered a swear word under her breath. "He tries to kiss me when she runs to the store."

I drew in a sharp breath. That old, old pain poked at tender spots inside me. "What do you do?"

"I don't do anything," she said angrily. "He just comes after me."

"Not to encourage him. That's not what I meant. What are you doing to stop him?"

"How could I stop him? He's a man. He's going to do whatever he wants to do. When I tried to tell Anna Joy, she called me a little tramp."

Painful memories criss-crossed each other. "Then move out."

"Where would I go?"

"I don't know. Your own apartment? Here? You could come to college."

"I've already been to jail. I don't think I could choose to go to another one."

"Then move out of Anna Joy's house. Get your own place."

Suzanne didn't answer and I realized she was silently crying. "Why do these things always happen to me?"

"I don't know. But I do know this. You have more options today than you will next week. And more choices next week than you will in a month. But you're the one who has to be strong here. No one can save you but yourself."

"You're naïve. You think this is simple. I can just pack up my suitcase and move into my own place."

"I didn't say it was simple or easy."

She didn't like my sermon and told me so. We walked back to the dorm without saying much more.

In the dorm, she chattered aimlessly with the other girls again. I tried to figure out why the others were drawn to her empty stories. She had a quick laugh, that was for sure. Was that what I'd always liked about her? That she liked me?

Sunday morning, she decided to take the early bus back to Wichita.

"I don't see any point in going to church."

I didn't try to talk her out of it because if the soul next to you on the pew is empty, it tends to empty you, too.

She left with her battered cardboard suitcase, leaning into the gray north wind, amidst circling, clattering leaves.

I never had a chance to tell her that Henry had written me twice.

— CHAPTER 18 —

I WENT HOME AT THANKSGIVING and again at Christmas, not minding going home or coming back.

Mama had stayed in mourning for Ben the whole time. She slipped deeper into her blue days, losing all that was sweet and light. Dad didn't talk much about the grayness in the house, but I did see both trips that he'd bought her flowering plants. Yellow mums in November, a brilliant red poinsettia at Christmas. The mums still bloomed then, as well as the geraniums Mama had potted up and carried over from October, so bright color patches dotted the house. But it wasn't enough. There could never be enough. It made me ache inside to be there.

Over Christmas, I baked carrot cookies and took some to the Fitches and the rest to Henry.

Martha hugged me and all the little ragamuffin boys dragged me in to see their prize possession: sleeping Sweetpea. Her plump, peach body lay swaddled in yellow blankets. The boys only breathed on her and whispered "shushshsh" to each other.

I left Martha at dusk and drove to the Schmidt farmstead. Henry was already finished choring and sitting at his kitchen table. Like he had the previous summer, he invited me in to share the cookies. I was ready this time. I put a little steel in my heart and said I had only a few days at home. I wanted to eat with Dad and Mama that night.

The cookies would bring another round of short letters from Henry, but I couldn't bear how lonely he must be these days. Marie had died on Christmas Eve. The last of his wayward daughters left just after New Year. His days had to be hollow and ringing with pain.

Of course, Ethel's world would be even worse. But I didn't want to think about her.

In late January, Henry wrote four lines on school tablet paper. I waited a few weeks and wrote back. The next time he wrote, his letter arrived the same day as an invitation and money for a bus ticket from Suzanne. The two of them—Henry and Suzanne—uncannily flowed in the same rhythm of loneliness. I didn't know if my well was deep enough for both—or even either of them. But I couldn't abandon them.

When I wrote back to Henry, I added that I was going to visit Suzanne. Pretending she didn't exist would only feed his illusion that somehow he'd just been dropped into his misery and not been party to the journey getting there.

I boarded the bus on a Saturday morning in March. I carried a heaviness in my stomach. It shouldn't be like this to visit a friend—if that's what we still were. I left my world of dove-white coverings and daily chapels and came into hers: noisy places and men in green and blue. It didn't matter that

Ben and Sam were cut from the same cloth as this. I'd stepped onto a different planet. The whole weekend I felt twisted up.

Suzanne and Anna Joy, who for the moment was Mrs. Burl Tweest, insisted we go out on Saturday night. I thought married military ladies were supposed to sit quietly at home and knit Red Cross bandages while their husbands went off to war. That's what *Life* magazine kept saying. But Anna Joy just splashed on some more lavender-scented toilette water and laughed at me.

Suzanne promised me I'd like going out. She loaned me a dress of hers and strappy black shoes. The only thing I can remember is that the dress was wildly red and flirted with my knees. Suzanne pulled my hair up into a collection of curls and painted my virgin lips ruby red and my eyelashes midnight black. Every mirror I passed that night I started at the stranger there.

"The band at this place is dreamy. They sound just like Harry James and His Orchestra," Suzanne promised. "You'll never want to listen to music on the radio again." She flashed her own ruby red lips at me.

We took two buses, I know that for sure, and ended up in a dance hall where smoke seemed to curl out of the windows and noise spilled out into the dusty street. We barely stepped in the door and Suzanne and Anna Joy swirled away with boys in uniform. I stood there, in my red dress and black shoe costume, ready to throw up, laugh hysterically, or cry. Maybe all three. Before I gave in to any one of them, a green-clad arm grabbed my elbow and tugged me out onto the dance floor. My body froze on me. I'd never so much as swayed to a gospel song. Around me, people jiggled and laughed. They threw their heads back and moved two to a single body, arms loose and wide.

The boy who grabbed me didn't notice I was a stick. He pushed and pulled and twirled me, then wrapped me in close to his body and kissed me. We were total strangers. I didn't even know his name. His hot breath smelled both sweet and sharp. I would have slapped him except we stayed within inches of each other.

This all had something to do with fear of death—his, maybe mine too—but I didn't understand why this excused a frenzy that suspended every other social convention. He didn't even notice that my eyes were huge circles. Or maybe he did and mistook the look for the magic of painted eyes.

The evening crept.

Every couple of songs, Suzanne or Anna Joy would bump into me, their eyes wild and faces flushed.

"Grand, isn't it?" they'd say and laugh, their breaths growing sharper and sweeter with the evening.

The smells, the music, the motion—all of them took me to a foreign place. Is this what Sam did every weekend? Had Ben? What would we even be able to talk about if they ever came home?

We slept late the next morning. I'd never done this— missing church because I was too lazy to get up. Anna Joy had already left to spend the day with friends. Suzanne made us some toast with white margarine.

"It's such a bother to mix in the packet of yellow coloring, so Anna Joy and I just eat it like this. If you shut your eyes, it tastes the same—bad!" We both laughed and groaned.

Suzanne crooned, "Baby, baby, baby! What's wrong with Uncle Sam? He's cut out all my bacon, now he's messin' with my ham."

We sat on the sun-warmed porch stoop off the kitchen, a place out of the way of the March breeze. It was an empty back yard, no trees or shrubs or flowers. Mama could never live here. I didn't think I could either.

"I hate this war," I said and sighed.

"Not me. I love it."

"How can you say that?"

"Easy. I'm making as much money as a man and every Saturday night is a party." She stretched out her bare legs and began untangling her curls with her fingers. "When the war ends, Burl will come home, and I'll be miserable in this house."

I didn't say anything. She'd heard my sermon once and didn't like it the first time. I asked her the old question again, though. "What will you do?"

She pulled her one shoulder up into a shrug. "It won't end tomorrow. I got time to think." She looked at me. "Your mama writes now and then." She paused to let that soak in. I'm sure she was watching for my expression. "She said I'd always be welcome to live with you all." Then she pulled a cigarette out of her pocket and lit it. Her lips left faint red lines on the brown cigarette paper.

"Mama'd sooner let chickens live in her house than a cigarette-smoking girl." I couldn't help it. It just slipped out.

Suzanne studied my face. "Then I guess I'd have to make a lot of excuses to go out behind the pig shed." She wrinkled up her nose and laughed. I did too.

"Mama's lonely."

"Aren't we all." She tapped her ashes onto the dirt, her arm in that distinctly Suzanne pose: arm and fingers straight, angled slightly out from her body. "Seems like we only lose the people in our lives, never gain."

"It doesn't have to be that way."

Suzanne didn't say anything or even look at me. Did she remember we'd already had this same conversation way back when in that other empty sunlit place? The yellow room where the girls all wore matching brown dresses and the mothers cried.

Suzanne drew in a deep breath through her cigarette then let the smoke stream out of her mouth.

"I saw your dad at Christmas."

"He still goes to church." Not a question. A statement from Suzanne to explain why I'd seen Henry.

"I took him some carrot cookies."

Suzanne hunched forward and wrapped her arms over her legs. She looked at my feet out of the corner of her eye. But she didn't say anything.

"He's very lonely."

"Aren't we all." She bit through the words this time. "Only difference is that he *chose* to be lonely." She puffed angrily on her cigarette. The ring of faint red lip lines grew darker.

"What choices are you making that will take you to a different place?"

Suzanne cocked her head farther and glared at me. "What are you talking about? Every choice I make is different than his."

"Yes." I felt impatient. No, angry. "But will they take you to a different end?"

The glare stayed.

"Tell me this. Is Anna Joy happier than your dad right now?"

Silence.

"Are you?"

"I thought you were my friend."

"I'm your best friend." *Maybe your only friend.* I studied my own feet. "That's why I have to ask you."

She blew out a final stream of smoke and smashed out her cigarette. A smooth, clean motion. So practiced. "I can never forgive him. He gave his daughters away. He could have stopped it from happening. But he let it happen again and again. He's evil, I tell you. Evil."

"Okay. Which one of you is telling the truth? You or Anna Joy?"

"What do you mean?" She thought it was a non sequitur, but it wasn't.

"Are you a tramp who's chasing her husband? Or is he a creep who tries to kiss you every time Anna Joy runs to the store?"

She chewed on her lip. "It's not the same. I could leave any time I want."

"But you haven't. And Anna Joy married Burl anyway."

Suzanne sat, eyes on the ground, arms locked around her knees. Finally, she said, "It's not the same." Her voice wavered. She was on the edge of tears.

"Maybe not. But it's still the same tangled knot. All of it."

She nodded. Tears tracked down her cheeks, taking some of last night's mascara with them.

"All I know is this. If you don't figure out how to let go of what your dad did—I'm not even saying he deserves it—but if you can't figure it out, you'll end up at the same place he is."

Or worse.

CHAPTER 19

Hester Prynne wore a scarlet A. I had *SIN, SIN, SIN* stamped on my forehead when I returned to campus that weekend. Fortunately, no one thought to read my forehead. I'd spent those thirty-six hours in closer proximity to decadence without slipping over the precipice than I thought humanly possible: smoking, drinking, dancing, swearing, kissing, cheating on marriage vows. There was probably also some real sex somewhere in there, but I was too naïve to see it.

Surely, Mama couldn't really be sincere about that invitation to Suzanne.

Suzanne didn't write for a while after that, but Henry did. The wheat looked good. The house seemed empty with Marie and the girls gone. It had rained a quarter inch. It could have been a Christmas letter. Just before the end of the semester, Suzanne wrote and invited me to come live with her and Anna Joy in Wichita for the summer. She'd get me a job at Boeing, and we'd have fun every Saturday night and sleep in on Sunday mornings. It wasn't for me, I knew that much. Fortunately,

LeRoy and Martha Fitch had already asked me to come back for the summer, so I could gracefully decline Suzanne's invitation. I'm sure, though, given the heightened state of her fall, it baffled her that I chose Sweethome over Wichita and five unruly boys and a Sweetpea instead of making lots of money and finding a party every Saturday.

That spring, the war tide had gradually shifted in our direction. In May, Allied troops broke through German defenses in Italy. In April, we surprised the Japanese on New Guinea. And in March we'd started bombing Berlin. If El Alamein had been the end of the beginning, we now had a sense that this, at least, was the beginning of the end.

Spring term ended and I packed my bags and returned home for the summer. My roommate, Pearl Shenk, returned to Cheraw, Colorado. We agreed that we would be roommates in the fall, but I told her to drink more milk and less Cheraw water. She thought that was funny and told me so in her loud, bossy way.

You never know what you should be thankful for until it's long past. Here we'd all brooded about Ben being lost—dead, imprisoned, forever gone—behind enemy lines. Then an ugly thing like the Normandy invasion comes along on June six, just days after the semester ended and weeks before harvest, and we all started breathing again since we knew for a fact he hadn't been killed on the shores of France or didn't have to kill a passel of Germans to survive. Dad turned on the radio that morning before Mama could get the Postum going and the corn mush sizzling. That's how we heard. It was dizzying. Edward R. Murrow told us that the ships dumped the American boys into the icy waters of the English Channel where they waded ashore into an enemy that spit fire at them. He made our boys sound bold, seasoned, steel-like. But we kept thinking, *Ben could have been there. Boys like Ben are there.* We'd never seen the ocean, never smelled or tasted or felt the pulsing power of it, but Mr. Murrow sculpted a vision so real that even on that hot June day in Kansas where the only oceans were made of wheat, I wanted a sweater. What rivers of blood flowed into and out of that ocean?

But for the moment, if Ben was still alive, then he was safe. The odd tension in that thought went unsaid.

I tried not to think about Sam. He'd stayed "desk-side," as he put it, up till now, doing lawyerly things as far as I could tell. But for something as huge and sweeping as this invasion, would they put everyone on a boat, trained or untrained, hardened or not? Maybe this was why the army couldn't afford to have the likes of even game-legged Buddy Holmes peeling potatoes at Camp Carson, since they might have had to round up all the potato peelers and put them on a boat, too.

The water sounded colder and the guns fiercer as the morning marched on. Mr. Murrow assured us that even though this invasion would leave a tidal wave of Allied bodies behind, we were winning it. I just kept having trouble understanding that. If Ben had been one of those who died in this invasion, how did we win? I wanted us to topple Hitler as surely as I wanted the wheat to grow, but I couldn't help but wonder whom the German mothers were listening to and what they were saying. Were the Axis radio folks saying the invasion would leave a tidal wave of bodies behind, but their boys were stopping the Allied advance? Did they know their sons' blood mingled with the blood of our sons? How many sonless mothers and fatherless children would today leave behind? How many aching hearts?

Finally, mid-morning I had to leave the radio. Mr. Murrow had done everything he could to lift our spirits, but to tell you the truth, the day just felt heavy. Maybe it was all those souls that had left their bodies, none of them buried, maybe most of them never would be. It seemed to tilt the earth's axis for a few hours, weighing down our very essence as humans.

Those first few weeks, the awful stories grew about this boy being killed or that one being maimed or these children losing their father. The sadness of it all stayed with us even though the *Sweethome Tribune* insisted that the Normandy invasion had been a good thing. We'd overwhelmed the Germans. The tide had mostly turned and now we were methodically rooting out the Germans. The end wasn't in sight yet, but now people had started to talk about "after the war." No one knew what it meant except that some kind of hope blossomed.

Martha Fitch and I would talk about it almost daily. She had a brother who was fighting in Italy, and so he'd escaped the horrors of Normandy. They hardly ever heard from him and when they did; he never wrote about anything of any substance. He could have been off cutting wheat in South Dakota for all there was to his letters. Either the war had made him hollow inside, or he was afraid that if they knew what it was like for him every day, they wouldn't be able to bear it. It sounded like Ben before he disappeared behind German lines. Both Martha and I wondered if we'd know anything more after they came home. If Ben came home.

My pattern from the previous summer repeated itself. In the morning, I'd crest the knoll above the Schmidt farmstead and see Henry standing in the door of the haymow. This summer he would usually look up at me, sometimes tilting his head up in acknowledgment, a few times giving a sharp hand motion that I suppose was a wave. Two summers in a row now, I'd seen him. How many mornings in between? How many mornings before that? He carried a demon with him.

That summer, LeRoy hooked up running water into the kitchen. Martha and I just giggled as we stood at the sink. We'd turn the faucet on, and water would come out of it! Then we'd turn it off, and the water would stop! The boys loved it. I badgered Dad about bringing plumbing into our house, but he just huffed a little at anything so frivolous on a farm. It didn't seem to make Mama much difference anyway. She mostly stayed out in her garden, tending roses and weeding rows and rows of gladiola bulbs and irises. It didn't look like she'd put out as many green beans or potatoes or tomatoes.

"What doesn't grow doesn't have to be canned," she told me one evening when the sunset colors layered on the horizon: black, then maroon, blood red, maroon again, dull gold, ivory, and blue. Ben had been a prisoner of war—or maybe worse, we never said it—for four hundred and eighty days. Four hundred eighty days of not knowing but thinking, of worrying, aching, and suffering. I knew because Mama wrote the days on the calendar above where she stacked the Bible and morning devotional booklet. She wrote that number at the end of the day, like she was giving the US Army the benefit of the doubt. If he showed up that day, she wouldn't count it as one of the days she'd lost. Being away at college had let that place in my heart scar over a little. Being at home opened the wound again, so a small part of me was sorry I hadn't gone to live in Wichita with Suzanne.

I baked a lot that summer in that magical Westinghouse stove, and I took to dividing my package that Martha always let me take home. If it was rolls, Henry got two. If it was near-sugarless cookies, he got four. He'd usually be in his kitchen beside the only dot of light in the house. He always invited me to stay, but I always declined. We'd talk for a few minutes, though. Sometimes we'd talk about the war. Mostly we talked about the weather and the crops. Kansas talk. When I told him about the Fitches' running water, he didn't huff at all. I guess that just goes to show you how desperate he was for a little companionship. We never talked about Suzanne or my visits with her. We seemed to have this unspoken understanding that we shouldn't pick at that scab.

— CHAPTER 20 —

WHEN SCHOOL STARTED AGAIN IN the fall, Pearl came back as promised. She knew more about Mexican boys and state fairs, and I knew more about running water. None of that did us much good in New Testament class, but she and I had some interesting conversations nevertheless.

One chilly November Saturday, Suzanne came for a visit. She came unannounced, not even a telegram. She just showed up in my dorm room. I came back from studying at the library and she was sitting on my bed, wearing her winter coat and those strappy black shoes she'd let me wear dancing the spring before. She looked sallow and frumpy, worse than I'd ever seen her, even in the scary days before her trial.

"Suzanne!"

"I wanted to get away. Is it okay if I stay for the weekend?"

"Surely. Are you all right?"

She nodded. But she didn't look all right. Her hair looked like it hadn't seen a comb in days, those ruby red lips like they'd been painted on slightly crooked. Her hands sat in her lap. She kneaded them over and over.

Pearl was two steps behind me and somehow missed the emptiness in Suzanne's face. "Girl, you look like you've slept under a boxcar."

Suzanne gasped a little and her eyes brimmed with tears.

"Don't pay any attention to her," I said to Suzanne. "Pearl's from Cheraw, remember? We think there's something in the water there, so she can't control the outlandish things that come out of her mouth."

Pearl laughed and poked her finger at me. "That's right. I even brought a five-gallon jug of it from home in case it starts to wear off." She dropped her books on her desk and opened the closet door. "Oh, no! It's gone! What will I ever do now?"

Suzanne smiled a little and took off her coat. She wore the red party dress she'd loaned me the spring before. Suzanne had always been the thinnest of the Schmidt sisters. Living with Anna Joy had somehow added a thickness to her body and the dress stretched uncomfortably tight from her bosom to her hips. Even her ankles looked puffy.

"Where's your suitcase?"

Suzanne slid one shoulder up and let it drop. "I didn't bring it."

"Didn't bring your suitcase—" Pearl began. I caught her eye and barely shook my head.

"It was just a spur of the moment decision to come." She looked at both of us. "There's a five o'clock bus back to Wichita. If I'm in the way, I can take that."

"Don't be silly. Why don't you go freshen up? We have to be in the dining hall in twenty minutes, so be quick." I loaned her a towel and soap. Pearl gave her a clean dress to put on, a dreary green stripe whose best feature was that it would fit Suzanne.

In spite of her Cheraw tendencies, Pearl didn't say any of the things that could be said, which only cemented our friendship more.

My table loved having Suzanne there. The quick bath and change of clothes had given a new glow to her charm. They couldn't see the emptiness in her banter because her smile was quick, and she brought a freshness to the table that drew others to her like miller moths to a light. There were funny stories about girls she worked with at Boeing and fretful stories about the boys she'd learned to know— she never explained how—who had gone off to fight in the war and had died or been maimed. She still had enough Mennonite in her, fortunately, to remember to sanitize everything that came out of her mouth. Tyrone Powers, lipsticks, and dreamy band music never came up once. Miss Shetler, our table matron, hardly had to furrow her brow at any of the stories.

After dinner, the two of us walked out into the country. A brisk north wind pushed us from the side. We could have had a gaggle of girls trail behind us, wanting to catch a little of the sparkle Suzanne left in her wake, but Pearl, bless her heart, distracted them until we were too far away for them to catch up without having to run and look silly.

Suzanne didn't say much. She waited until we were well beyond the first farmer's hedgerow before she pulled out her cigarettes. A fringe of Pearl's dowdy green-striped dress stuck out below Suzanne's coat. I tried not to think about Pearl's reaction if the dress came back with little ash burns. It was only after she'd taken a deep drag or two on her cigarette that her thoughts started to tumble out.

"Burl came home yesterday." The cigarette arm stood out at the peculiarly Suzanne angle. The wind swirled the ashes off the end and kept it sharply glowing.

"Anna Joy's husband?"

She nodded.

"I thought he'd been shipped off."

"Omaha Beach," she said succinctly. "It was a bloodbath. He lived but his left leg and arm got all shot up. He's been convalescing in an army hospital in New Jersey all this time. Now that he can kind of walk again, they're done with him. They put him on a train and sent him back to Wichita."

She took another long drag on her cigarette. "Anna Joy got the telegram he was coming home, but never told me. I walked in the door and he was sitting at the kitchen table, a whiskey bottle in one hand and cigarette in the other. Just like old times." She mimicked the stance as though I wouldn't be able to picture it.

"What—" I began, but she didn't let me finish.

"First thing he says to me is 'Come over here little Suzy Q and give your brother a big smooch.' First thing." She shook her head and rubbed her forehead with her free hand. "Simon used to call me Suzy Q. Did I ever tell you that?" She took a deep breath and shook her head again. "All those good boys that died at Normandy. Why didn't the Germans get one of the bad ones?"

I kept my mouth shut. None of the things that came to mind sounded like something a friend would say.

"I went to my room and slammed the door and got ready to go out for the evening. When I left, Anna Joy didn't look none too happy about being stuck at home. But she was the one who married him." She tapped another cigarette out of the pack and lit it off the first one, then dropped that one, still burning, on the road. "I didn't go home. I went out dancing then went to the bus station and waited for the first bus here. I don't know what I'll do. I can't go back there."

I didn't know how I was supposed to fix all of this. She never listened to me. Whatever ideas I had weren't the ones she wanted to hear. "What about some of the girls you work with at Boeing? Can't you move in with one of them?"

She shook her head and rolled her eyes.

"How about your own place? Aren't you making enough money to do that?"

She chewed her lower lip and stared at the horizon. "For now, maybe."

"Do it then. The war won't end tomorrow. You'll have time to figure out something before a man comes home and takes your job."

"Cat." She stopped walking and turned to face me. "I'm pregnant. I thought maybe you'd figured that out. I can only hide it awhile longer before my boss finds out, and then I won't have a job anymore."

"You're pregnant? You're not married, how could you be—" I blushed, my face hot against the cool north wind.

She just kept staring at me. "Maybe you didn't know this, but you don't have to be married to get pregnant."

"What about the father? Surely . . ." even as I talked I knew there was nothing "surely" about it. He was probably some military boy who'd been shipped off and killed.

Suzanne tightly wrapped her one arm over her body. Her other one still angled downward with the cigarette glowing at the end. She looked down at her strappy black dancing shoes. Dust from a Kansas back-country road covered them now. "I don't know who the father is."

I sucked in my breath. "You don't know which boy is the father or you don't know the name of the boy?" Either thought was full of too many awful possible stories.

She threw down the cigarette and covered her face with her hand. The other arm still wrapped her body. "Maybe both." She cried now in long, hard sobs that shuddered her body uncontrollably. "It's so broken, it'll never be fixed again."

I should have wrapped my arms around my friend, but I was too stunned. What she'd just told me was so far out of my reality that I could only stand there in the wind, my arms wrapped around my own body. I tried to breathe. I tried to think. But I could only remember all the sad things that had brought us to that moment.

My college education failed me. There was nothing from English, Bible, Latin, biology, or Western civilization that gave me the right thing to say at the moment. Of all the useless classes, Western civ won the award. Think of it. Thousands of years of history and not one sensible response to my pregnant friend. Unfortunately, this bit of newly found wisdom wouldn't do me any good on Monday morning at eleven either. But I tucked it away anyway.

"I just don't understand. How could you have . . . have . . ." I didn't know any of the right words to ask the questions.

"Don't you think I ask myself that every day? All I know is that this isn't who I want to be. But it's too late."

"What are you going to do?"

"About the baby? I don't know. Anna Joy says she knows this girl who knows someone who knows a doctor who'll help me."

"Why are you worried about a doctor to deliver it now?"

Suzanne chewed on her fingernail and looked at her feet. "It's not that kind of doctor."

"What do you mean? What other kind of doctor would you need?"

She didn't say anything. She just glanced up at me and then down at her feet again.

I grabbed her arms. "Look at me, Suzanne. What are you talking about? How would this doctor 'help you'?"

"Never mind. I'm sorry I brought it up. I'm sorry I told you anything." She was back to tears again. "You live in this little cocoon and you always have. Maybe I've always wanted to be your friend because I wanted to live in that cocoon, too. Only now I've figured out that could never happen. I've ruined all my chances to ever be that way." She pulled away from me and started back down the road toward town. "I'd be better off dead. This baby would be better off dead." She stopped and turned back to me. "That's what this doctor could do."

"What?" The horror of this idea had a physical presence. Its weight settled over me so that my legs and arms were too heavy to move.

"You heard me. That's what this doctor could do."

I needed some place other than the middle of a dirt road to sit down. My knees, my ankles wouldn't hold me much longer. "And you'd want that on your shoulders, too?" I think I was shouting. If this is what she'd come to, I could never help her because she didn't really want to be helped. "Going to this . . . this doctor will only take care—no, it won't take care of this problem. It'll change the problem. Instead of having to deal with a child and no husband, you'll have to live with taking a life." And then I said the most dangerous thing: "*Another* life."

She stopped walking.

"That's right. When you pushed Simon, it didn't take care of the problem. It only changed the problem. You might have saved dozens of other girls from Simon, but you didn't save yourself."

She turned and looked at me. Tears smeared her face. "I can't go backwards. I don't know how to undo any of that."

"You can't. But you don't have to add another layer to it."

She just kept shaking her head and crying. "There's no way out of this mess."

"You could go live with Dad and Mama. They'd take you in." It was a wild idea for all sides. What would Dad do with a pregnant, unmarried girl living in his house, even if he'd known her since infancy? But maybe it would revive Mama, give her something to nurture besides roses.

"And be a section away from Pops? Never!" She shivered. "I'd sooner go to that doctor and be done with it."

"But if—"

"I will never live near that awful hole of a place again. Never!"

"What about Edwin and Tilly? Or Tim and Inez?" I tried to think. "What would Dess tell you to do?"

"Dess? You think this is the same thing as Dess?' She spat out the words. "What don't you understand? No one came sneaking into my bed at night. No one forced himself on me. No one—" She grabbed me by the shoulders and shook me. "Cat. Look at me. I'm in the most shameful condition a girl can find herself. Do you know how much courage it took to come here? To see you?" I could hardly understand her because she was sobbing so hard. "If Burl hadn't come home, maybe you wouldn't have ever found out either." She buried her face in her hands. "I would have just killed myself and been done with it."

I finally wrapped my arms around her and let her cry. I wanted to tell her that we'd figure out something, but I didn't believe it myself. It was one thing to have saved Suzanne from the noose. But I'd have to become the Queen of Hearts herself to believe this impossible thing: that I could save Suzanne from herself.

CHAPTER 21

THAT YEAR, THANKSGIVING WASN'T FOR sissies. There was hardly a soul left in America who didn't have a brother, a father, a child, cousin, neighbor, or friend fighting, wounded, killed, or—like us—missing in action. Even in the staunchest Mennonite communities where they excommunicated boys who went into the military, everyone knew and cared about someone who might not ever come home again. And if they didn't have one of their own, lots of Mennonites still had recent Dutch, German, or Russian roots. Everyone worried about cousins or even siblings over there, and what they remembered of their childhoods that might have been destroyed.

It wasn't just Mennonites who still had tentacles in Europe. Ironically, it seemed half the country was first- or second-generation still, so they worried about their own sons who had to go off and fight cousins in Germany or Italy.

I took the bus back to Sweethome for the holiday weekend, even though the bus company continued to firmly tell people not to travel since they already had enough passengers—mostly soldiers—hanging out the windows and didn't have room for the rest of us. I rode in a sea of green, pressed against legs and arms. Something about the war had loosened social inhibitions because those boys whistled and flirted like they hadn't seen a girl in a coon's age even though they'd all probably kissed one the night before and would kiss a different one that night.

We went to Uncle Emery's for Thanksgiving, but it felt odd somehow since none of the cousins from a distance could come. They had to save their gas coupons for running tractors and going into town for supplies. Mama didn't want to go. She just wanted to stay home in bed, where apparently she'd been spending a lot of her days. After the last hard frost she didn't have much reason to be in the garden except to clean up dead plants, and she couldn't do that right now, not with so much hollowness already. But Dad managed to badger her into going to Emery's. He kept saying it would be good for her to get out and be with people more, so she went, but the whole day she looked like she was somewhere else.

I'd wanted desperately to talk to her about Suzanne. I knew she could keep the secret, and even if she didn't have any ideas, just by talking to her, I might figure out some way to help Suzanne. Now I knew that Mama couldn't carry one more burden, even if it was someone else's child. She was broken. I didn't know if she could endure one more season of waiting to know about Ben, and it could be many seasons.

The Allies seemed to be stamping out the war on the European front like you would a bad fire. They were bringing it down to a smolder, but every so often another little fire would flare up. Just a month earlier, the Polish underground had risen up against the German occupiers. In retaliation, rumor had it that the Germans killed hundreds of thousands of Poles and leveled the city. Which always left this question: what would they do to one poor Kansas farm boy who never should have been there in the first place? We never asked those questions out loud.

On Friday, I saddled up Little Willy and headed across the fields of winter wheat to the Fitches'. As I crossed the knoll on the Schmidt place, I could hear Henry banging milk cans around in the barn, a lonely sound that called out for some human contact. Thanksgiving must have been flat and unbearable for him: no wife, no daughters, no grandchildren. No warmth or talking or encouraging. No one to say, *At least we have each other.* One day would be like the last for him, and the next.

And then Ethel crossed my mind. I didn't like thinking about her. I *never* wanted to feel a grain of sympathy for her. I wanted her to be miserable.

It always seemed like a body's best inspiration should come on a Sunday morning just after a rousing sermon while you're down on your knees in prayer. For me, it just never happened like that, though. That weekend, my best inspiration came sitting at Martha Fitch's kitchen table. The wind puffed in fits outside, but the sun baked down and raised the temperature to degrees just above freezing. It wasn't blizzarding and there wasn't a tornado or a bolt of lightning in sight, which meant it was a nice enough day for the herd of Fitch boys to play outside. Those boys had corrupted little Sweetpea, so mostly she just toddled around the kitchen and hung by the back door, saying, "Out? Out?" Only sixteen months old and she already understood that girls were born to be trapped inside the kitchen while the boys got to be outside in the dirt.

Martha ignored Sweetpea's descant better than I could. Maybe it was the thought of Suzanne. A year from now she'd have her own baby, but no husband, no job, no family to help her. Katie Fast and her squalor of babies. It made me weak to think about it. But Martha was chattering on about twin stuff. "And to think, my poor sister Mona Beeb's never had a one."

"No twins?" I loved Martha, truly like a sister, but I was only half listening.

"No twins. No babies. No nothing. I thought I'd told you about her." Martha just shook her head. "She and that husband of hers only got that passel of cats, but it ain't the same, and she knows it."

My heart stopped. "Does she want children?"

"Oh, honey, she aches to have children. It's the saddest thing in the world to watch. Sometimes I just feel bad to have so many sweet things, and she don't have a one."

I fluttered inside.

"Honestly, Cat, she'd rob a bank to get one if that's where they kept babies."

"She doesn't have to rob a bank."

Martha laughed. "I know that. But I'm just saying that she'd do something crazy if that's what it took."

"Would she be a good mama?" I have to admit I wasn't even sure I cared about the answer.

Martha didn't pause a beat. "Well, she takes good care of all those cats."

"It's not exactly the same thing," I said.

"No, no. I know that. But she just . . . she's wanted a baby for so long that I can't imagine that she wouldn't love that baby to pieces."

"Then I might just have an idea."

We hatched this wonderful plan. Suzanne could go live with Mona Beeb in Wynona, Oklahoma. Mona Beeb would keep the baby. Suzanne would recover her dignity. The baby would have a daddy and a mama.

Maybe it wouldn't be too late for any of them.

It had to be an absolute secret, though. No one from Sweethome could ever find out where this baby came from. We were both so excited that we wrote letters to Suzanne and Mona Beeb right there and then.

Hope.

The morning invigorated me. For the first time since Suzanne's visit, I wasn't weighed down.

If only it could have been so easy with Mama. Or Ethel.

CHAPTER 22

YOU KNOW HOW A WEED will find any crack in a sidewalk? It'll just start pushing its way up right in the middle of where it's not supposed to be, against all logic in nature. That's what Ethel was doing. She'd become the weed in my sidewalk, inserting herself into my thoughts against all logic. This woman was nothing to me. First of all, she wasn't likable. And when I'd lived with her and Simon for those few long weeks years ago, she would have as easily let me become another victim as not. She was nothing to me.

So why did that weed grow?

I wondered that as I sat in church with Mama the Sunday after Thanksgiving before I caught the bus back to Hesston. I guess I'd never realized it before, but Mama's habitual pewspot was only two rows behind Ethel's and just to the right. Which meant that to pay any attention to Brother Bender's sermon, I had to watch Ethel's slightly upward tilt in her nose. Sunday after Sunday, year after year, that's what Mama had done. Through the parade of girls with unhappy stories, the Ben years, the attempt to throw Brother Edwin out of the pulpit, and the murder trial—Mama had been close enough to reach over and pat Ethel on the shoulder.

After the church service, I stayed with Mama for the ladies' Sunday school class. The men stayed on one side of the sanctuary but circled in closer around their teacher. The women did the same on their side. Both Ethel and Henry seemed to have unseen fences around them. They were invisible. Henry reached out and shook a few hands, but no one reached out to Ethel. Even the phone-perching Wenger twins, who would've gossiped with a fly on the wall, didn't seem to notice Ethel that morning. She didn't really look people in the eye either but finally drifted over to her car and left. Henry stood on the edge of conversation circles for a while and then he, too, got into his car. At one point, he'd caught my eye and smiled and nodded slightly, but he never tried to come over and talk. Maybe he thought the contact would taint me, and I'd end up with my own invisible fence.

There are different kinds of sadnesses. Some are thrust on you and some you choose. The trouble is, even when you think it's been thrust on you, often you've really chosen it. But you can't tell people that. They have to figure it out for themselves.

I didn't hear from Suzanne again until just before Christmas. The postmark on the letter was from Wynona, Oklahoma.

> *My Dearest Cat,*
> *Merry Christmas!! How can I ever ever thank you enough? Mona Beeb and Charlie are the sweetest,*

kindest people in the whole world. I don't know which one of us is the happiest that I'm here. Hardly a day goes by that one of us doesn't end up crying a little about it because we're so happy. Even Charlie!! (He's a real hoot!) I can finally feel excited about my condition, not because I got into this mess, but because there really will be some good that comes out of it. Mona Beeb and Charlie will be wonderful parents!!! They say they'll let me come back and see the baby whenever I want.

Burl didn't want me to come here. He said I could stay with him and Anna Joy forever and he'd take care of us both. And then he said both of us could take care of him and he winked. (You know what he meant!) Can you believe that!! He's such a feckless creep!!! I'm glad I'm out of there, but I feel sorry for Anna Joy. She's got a real bad one this time.

I know cats are the ones that are supposed to have 9 lives. But you, dear friend, keep giving me one of yours. You've saved me over and over. I made a promise to myself that this would be the last time. I'm going to stop fooling around and get my life together.

Love,

Suzanne

I really wanted to believe her. I really did.

I couldn't quite name the feeling I had about going home for Christmas. All I knew was that as the time got closer, I felt more anxious, almost sad. I was glad to take a break from school, but home had turned into this empty, dark place. Dad met me at the bus in Sweethome. He'd never been the talker in our family anyway, and now, with Mama so blue all the time, he seemed to have lost the ability to make simple conversation. I tried to talk, but as it goes when the conversation is only one-sided, what I said was just mindless chatter.

When we turned onto the road for our lane, he finally interrupted me. "It's going to be real good to have you home." His voice was thick and a little hoarse, maybe from emotion, maybe from so little use. "Mama just don't seem to have her same spirit about her. She'll never get over losing Ben."

"But we don't know for sure that he's dead."

"Six hundred and thirty days, Kittycat. Anymore, that's worse than dead for her." We pulled into the lane and Dad turned off the car, but neither of us made a move to get out. "What's he had to be living with? What are those Nazis doing to him?"

I never let myself think about that and I didn't want to now, either. Dad's cheeks were wet.

"I don't know how much longer we'll be able to keep her."

"Mama? What are you saying?"

He nodded and his face crinkled up in tears and emotions. "She's sad. She's just real sad all the time." His shoulders shook. "She can't seem to get out of bed or get herself dressed. I try to fix her a little food and she won't eat it." He got out his bandana and blew his nose. "They'd never count her as part of a statistic, but this war has wounded her as surely as if a Nazi had shot her in the heart." As we pulled into the lane, he said, "Maybe you shouldn't go back to college."

An arrow pierced my stomach. "What are you saying?

"She'd be better if you were here at home."

I took a deep breath. I couldn't believe what he'd just asked me to do. "Then that would be three of us lost to the war." My voice shook as I said it, and I wondered what guilt I'd live with for saying it.

If only it had been May. We could have gathered an armful of lilacs before walking in the door. But it was December.

Mama lay in her darkened bed, her face colorless against the late-afternoon light. Her long, thick night braid barely hung together. I don't know how many nights it had been since she'd braided it. She didn't appear to be sleeping, more just staring, looking ever so much like she was laid out in a casket.

Had this been a dream at one time, too? I couldn't remember.

"Mama?" It was all I could say. Anything more and I'd burst into tears. While it was true she hadn't looked much better at Thanksgiving, at least then she'd met me in the kitchen and had cooked supper.

"Cat?" She smiled. "What are you doing here?"

I breathed a couple of times to control the emotion in my voice. "It's my Christmas break, Mama. Remember? I'll be here until after New Year's."

"Well that's wonderful." She smiled but didn't move.

I looked at Dad, who had stayed by the door. He just shook his head. A helpless motion.

"You're looking too thin, Cat."

I laughed nervously. "We're all too thin. It's the war. There's nothing to eat."

She smiled again.

"Mama. Why don't you come sit with me in the kitchen, and I'll bake us some bread. Last I heard, the government hadn't taken flour away from us."

"Shhh." She said it like she would have to me in church a decade earlier. "Don't give them any ideas!"

"Will you come sit with me?"

She sighed. "Well, I'm pretty tired right now. I just don't seem to have the energy I used to. Maybe later."

"Rose, you ought to get up. Cat's not here long enough for you to lollygag in bed."

I cringed at lollygag, but Mama didn't seem to notice the word. She looked past me to Dad. "Did we hear anything about Ben today, Ezra?"

Behind me, Dad sighed long and deep. "Not today, Rose. But I'm sure we'll hear soon. The war keeps winding down. The radio says surrender is just around the corner."

Mama nodded slightly.

Dad and I left the room and went to the kitchen. I started the yeast softening in warm milk and gathered the rest of the ingredients.

"She's much worse than she was at Thanksgiving."

Dad shook his head. "She managed to get out of bed more that weekend, but she's been like this most of the fall."

"Have you taken her to the doctor?"

Dad shrugged a shoulder. "He wasn't any help. He said it was woman troubles. But it ain't. It's losing Ben the way we did."

"We don't know that he's gone for good." I wanted him to stop talking like Ben was dead.

Dad didn't say anything, but he drummed his fingers on the table. The calendar behind him had a number scrawled in each day's box, easily more than half in Dad's handwriting. Were those the days Mama had never made it out of bed? Yesterday's read *629*. He'd already counted today. He knew the government wouldn't be bringing any news to us.

"I thought maybe she'd perk up a little more with you home." Dad's face looked as drawn and ashen as Mama's. "If we can just get her out of bed every day, that would be a start."

I was kneading the bread when he said this. I was just glad I had something to pound and push.

"Maybe you could take her into town. Except for when I can get her to go to church, she hasn't been into Sweethome for months."

"I could take her over to see Martha one day. Those little boys are real livewires. And she'd love Sweetpea."

"We just have to get her out of bed every day. When she gets up and gets dressed, she's a little better for a while."

I set the dough in the oven to raise, then started cleaning the kitchen. Dad had put food away and washed the dishes, but it didn't look like the floor had seen a mop or the shelves a damp rag for a month. He pumped some fresh water for me and kept me company the whole time. Back then, those two things would have been the man's job in the kitchen. Neither of us thought a whit about it. By the time the bread was baking, the kitchen felt less gritty and more like you could really cook in it again.

"I sometimes wonder what Henry Schmidt does," Dad said out of the blue. "How does he ever get his house clean?"

"He doesn't. Whenever I've stopped by, the place is filthy. You'd hate to go barefoot in the house."

Dad just shook his head. "I don't know how he gets through his days. Chasing off his daughters like he did. Marie gone. What would he have to live for?"

"I don't know. I can't imagine that either."

"Is Suzanne still at Boeing there in Wichita?"

My stomach tensed. "She quit. I'm not sure what she's doing for work right now." It wasn't quite a lie, but for all practical purposes it had the same affect.

"She still living with Anna Joy?"

How did we get down this conversation path? It was full of dangerous possibilities. "She . . . uh . . . moved out. She said Anna Joy's husband was flirting with her. Always wanted to kiss her. That sort of thing." I was glad I was cleaning a high shelf. Dad couldn't see my face go red.

"No!"

I nodded. "It's the truth. Suzanne said that Anna Joy just called her a little tramp and said she was to blame for it."

"Was she?"

It was a fair question, especially given her current state. I didn't know how she might tease a boy these days. "I don't know. But it kind of strikes me that Anna Joy didn't want to know the truth, just in case she'd have to throw out a bad husband."

"It never changes, does it? A body just sees what they want to see."

"Anna Joy doesn't seem in any good shape either." I desperately wanted to keep Dad from asking his next question about Suzanne. "She's out there cattin' around. Makes you wonder."

There was silence behind me. Finally, Dad just said, "It surely does."

It blew something fierce the Sunday before Christmas. The wind whistled down from the Dakotas, bringing nearly invisible snowflakes that gathered and gathered until white shadows laced every north face. We bundled up for church, somehow coaxing Mama out of her toasty bed, and cautiously drove the miles into town, sliding along the blacktop highway and gripping on the gravel shoulders when the tires slipped toward the ditches. Nothing ever mattered on a Sunday morning. Unless a body couldn't dig themselves out of a drifted-in lane or someone had died, sooner or later, they'd be sitting in a pew.

Even Ethel somehow managed to show up that Sunday, and she hadn't learned to drive until after Simon was gone.

There was that weed again. Pushing its way up in the middle of winter.

Being that it was Christmas season and all, the primary department dressed in gauzy capes and tinsel wings and sang sweetly about silent nights and mangers and heralding angels. Little Moses Smallbrook would have been among them, but Tim, Inez, and Dess hadn't darkened the church door in so long that little Moses might not even know about Baby Jesus if his household were careless.

If Henry's thoughts drifted in the same direction, he masked it well.

After church, I watched Henry and Ethel inside their unseen fences again. Unexpectedly, something moved inside me, though, and I interrupted Ethel's invisible journey down the center aisle.

"Ethel. How are you doing?"

I startled her, I could tell.

"I'm fine." She looked ready to dart away.

"Those surely were bad roads this morning, weren't they?"

"My goodness gracious yes. I nearly landed in the ditch twice." She shuddered. "I shoulda turned around and gone back home, but I was too scared." She rattled out her words fast, like she wasn't used to talking.

"Maybe the sun will have melted a little off in the last few hours."

"Oh, let's hope so."

I fell along side her in the aisle. "Will all your children be home for Christmas this year?" It was an unchristian question, but I couldn't help myself.

She shook her head slightly. Her jowly cheeks quivered with the movement. "Oh, not this year. With the war on and everything, they have to be careful about their gas coupons."

I was pretty sure that Harold, the slouching boy now slouching man, still lived no more than a couple gallons away. "That's too bad." We shuffled along, waiting for people to finish conversations and move a little further and faster. "Will you be alone this Christmas?"

She nodded but didn't look up. "I'm afraid so. Won't be the first time."

"It must be hard, being alone on holidays like that."

If she thought we were enemies, she didn't show it, but then that probably just goes to show you what a demon loneliness can be.

"It is. Holidays are the worst." She shook her head. "Thanksgiving, I'd like to've cried all day long."

"Cat!" One of the Unruh twins grabbed my elbow and pulled me into her pew. "It's wonderful to see you!"

Ethel finally looked at me, but didn't make any effort to keep me talking to her. I hadn't missed either of the Unruh twins as long as I'd been away, but I was glad for the excuse to escape Ethel. We were only headed toward dangerous waters.

The twin chattered aimlessly, I think about her new watch, which was a Mennonite engagement ring. Some boy from over by Hutchinson had fallen for her while following the harvest. Now that she'd caught him, she wanted him snagged for good. I forgot to ask what he was doing following the harvest instead of getting drafted. By the time I acted sufficiently happy for her and untangled myself, Ethel was long gone. It wasn't like I was going to invite her for Christmas dinner, but I wasn't exactly done talking to her either. Now I'd be the one to use some coupons.

I hoped it would be worth it.

━━ ❧ ═══ CHAPTER 23 ═══ ❧ ━━

THE LAST TIME I'D BEEN to Ethel Yoder's farm, the barn had been redder, the house bigger, and my soul closer to being stolen. Simon had kissed me that week. He'd touched secret places on my body and bought me a beautiful pink blouse. If Granddad hadn't died that weekend, it would have been only days—a week or two at most—and Simon would have taken me down a path I couldn't have returned from.

I had to drive past the Yoder lane twice before I could bring myself to turn in. Even as I did, my head flooded with princess rooms and Ben and his thumping basketball in the barn. Simon was dead now. But the flash of his golden smile, his wink, his lingering scent all crept into the car with me.

I wanted to cry. Life had traveled so far in the last seven years. I couldn't forget why I'd come.

I carried my precious package of cinnamon rolls to the kitchen door and knocked.

I'd been here another time, too, much longer ago. Dad had set me on a wooden chair in the middle of a chaotic kitchen while Simon maneuvered to make Dad believe he

190

could save our farm. A bankerman died only hours later. My knees grew weak. I wanted to sit down now.

"Catherine?" She said it as she opened the door. There was no mistaking her surprise.

"Merry Christmas, Ethel." I handed her the cinnamon rolls.

"For me?" Her lips pinched together like old times. She would never learn to look gracious.

"Yes. After we talked on Sunday, I got to thinking. It must be lonely out here with none of your children to visit on the holidays. I wanted to bring you a little something." Every word held truth, even if they implied a different purpose than the one I held.

She looked wary. She should have. She held the fresh cinnamon rolls.

They came with a price, but I'm not sure she understood how stiff the price was. Then again, loneliness will drive a body to all kinds of bad judgment.

"Why don't you come in. That wind'll whip right into your bones if you stand out there long enough." She pushed the screen door open for me.

I stepped inside, and the years just disappeared. Simon could have come whistling around the corner, and I wouldn't have blinked. The kitchen looked pretty much like it had the first time I'd ever come. Dishes filled the sink; shabby piles of this and that covered the table and tiny counter space. Even the refrigerator had yellowing stacks of stuff. She cleared a spot for me to sit. I half expected her to offer me a couple of stale sugar cookies and bring out the flannel board and the Bible people.

"Pardon my mess. I just haven't had time to clean." She said it apologetically, but it was a ludicrous thing to say: she didn't have a husband, children, hobby, or job. It was winter. It wasn't like she'd been working in her garden since she didn't do that even in the summer.

"Would you like some water? Or maybe some coffee? I still have some coffee."

The offer was seductive, but I didn't want to feel kindly toward her in any way beyond what I already did. A cup of real coffee, one that didn't taste like Postum's bitter burnt roots, might soften my heart. How could I be direct if she'd sacrificed a ration coupon for me? Humans are so easily bought.

"No, thanks. A glass of water would be fine." I lied, but it was a small lie.

Ethel opened and shut cabinet doors, looking for a real glass without a chip and not a jelly jar. Finally, she settled for a jelly jar without a chip. While she knocked around her cabinets, I closed my eyes so I could remember why I'd come.

Katie Fast had cooked in this kitchen. So had Ada Harder and Myrtle Unruh. And all of the Schmidt girls except for Emily. Selma Lichti took her own life upstairs at the end of the hall. In the bedroom above me, Simon had changed them all forever, never by their own choosing. I was sure of that.

"You okay?" Ethel set the water on a tiny open space on the table. I could hear anxiety rising in her voice. It has its own rhythm and pitch.

I nodded but was afraid to talk because of what she might hear in my own voice.

Ethel had never been a talker and had had even less practice in the last few years. Still, she gave it her best shot.

"How's your mama doing?"

"She's awful sad."

"She don't look good on Sundays. I never know whether it's better to keep quiet or to say something."

I shook my head. That one didn't have an answer.

"You folks ever hear anything more about what might have happened to him?"

I shook my head. "Dad and I keep praying he's alive. Mama just keeps praying." Even as I said it, I knew it wasn't true.

"It ain't easy to lose a child."

"That's for sure." I let the comment settle. I could have run at the mouth about the kind of emptiness that comes over you when part of your flesh is stolen from you like that, but I thought more would come of our visit if I didn't talk. Most people can't stand silence. They'd rather offer all kinds of foolish information than listen to the clock ticking in the next room, even if that's what they've done day in and day out for years.

"Harold got drafted." The slouching boy. It must have happened early on in the war. He was a good eight or ten years older than me. "They didn't take him, though. Said he had flat feet. I was surely glad about that." No mention of whether he would have claimed to be a conscientious objector. Maybe that omission held a shadow of integrity since it probably wouldn't have been true.

"What's Harold doing these days?"

Reflexively, her brow furrowed deep then she tried to smile, but it was too late. "Oh, he's in between jobs right now."

"Oh?" The war ensured that only the mentally infirm and cripples didn't have jobs that year.

Ethel shifted in her seat. Her forehead glistened slightly even though it wasn't hot. "He was working at the elevator over in Coldwater. His boss got after him for flirting with his girls. It was a harmless thing, but the boss didn't like it and let him go." She shook her head slightly like she hadn't really convinced herself. "It was just harmless. He didn't mean anything by it."

It was amazing what a pan of cinnamon rolls could buy.

"I'm sure he'll find something soon. Lotta jobs out there and not enough bodies these days."

"Oh, uh-huh." She looked distracted, like she'd lost her train of thought. "He . . . uh—" This time she mopped her brow with her apron skirt. "Well, he's in a bit of a fix right now. They got him sitting in jail."

For flirting? My eyes widened, I know. "That must be awfully hard on you." I avoided asking any questions, but it was killing me.

"It's terrible hard without Simon here to fix things. I just don't know what to do."

"Does he have a lawyer?" Surely, that wasn't prying too much.

She nodded. "He's used him before, so I know he's a good one."

More revelations. This news should have had a sweeter taste, but I can't say that it did. Ethel looked old and shriveled and empty. She'd made a lot of bad choices in her lifetime. Given a chance, I don't know if she would have made a single one differently, but at that moment, I still felt sorry for her. Having a child who turns out to be a bad weed is sad even if you were the one who planted him.

"Are any of your girls around to help?"

Another involuntary frown. She pinched her lips tighter and shook her head. "Oh, they're busy with their own troubles."

"I don't even know, do they live close?"

She shook her head again. "Helen's the closest. She's all the way over at Tulsa. Has two little rascals and another on the way. Not one of the girls has been home since the funeral." She looked at the floor and sighed deeply.

"Well, there are a lot of ways to lose a child these days."

"Ain't that the truth." She nodded and said it again, this time more to herself than me. "Ain't that the truth."

It would have been easier to leave then, but then my trip over here would have been a waste of a gas coupon and a little sugar. Besides, she kept opening the door wider.

"When Simon was alive, I had everything. Now I have nothing. I don't know how this happened."

"Really?" It just popped out of my mouth, and I was immediately sorry. I wanted to be more measured in what I said to her. I guess it's always easier to look at someone else's troubles and be wise, but it was hard to understand how she could have been near dead center in Simon's vortex and not see how he wrecked lives. Here she sat, in her messy kitchen, without children to speak of or friends to visit, and she still hadn't connected the dots. There were so few dots to connect that I tensed up. Emotion bubbled up inside me, and I didn't want it to. I wanted to have a careful conversation with Ethel, and I didn't want it colored by the flecks of rage that would surely rise to the surface.

Ethel studied me. Her lips pinched tight.

"Ethel." I kept my voice soft and gently put my hand on her forearm. "Put the puzzle pieces together. Look at what Simon did to the hired girls. Look at what he did to your girls." It was a leap, a risky assumption since I only suspected the Yoder girls' lives ran parallel to the sad lives that the hired girls lived.

She stiffened but didn't jerk her arm away. She probably hadn't been touched in a month of Sundays. When you're starving, it's easy to compromise yourself.

"How dare you come to my house and talk that way about my Simon?"

My Simon.

I took a deep breath.

"Ethel. 'Your' Simon kissed me when I was twelve years old. He touched me in places no man should ever touch a little girl."

Now she jerked her whole body away from me. "Stop it."

I shook my head. "No, Ethel. What he did to me was nothing. Nothing, I tell you. Dess has his baby. You know this. Little Moses is Simon's son."

"Stop it! Stop saying those awful things." She scooted her chair back so fast she nearly tipped over.

"How many other girls had his baby? How many girls wish they were dead because of Simon?"

"You're horrible! Horrible!"

"Ethel." I kept my voice low and soft, battling against every urge in my body. "I didn't come here to be horrible. Don't you realize that until you can be honest about what happened, nothing can change for any of those girls? For your own children?" I sighed. "For you."

"It's not true. None of it's true about my Simon." She mopped her forehead with her apron and then buried her face in her aproned hand. Her shoulders shook with tiny sobs.

"It is true. And saying it's *not* won't change anything."

"It's all lies," she said fiercely. "All those girls are telling the most awful lies. They lied at the trial and they're still lying. Dess is the most horrible liar of them all, saying that about Moses. My Simon had a heart of gold. There wasn't anyone in three counties as generous as him."

I shook my head and took another slow, deep breath. "He was generous. I'm sure some of it was just because he honestly wanted to help people out. But sometimes it was because he was buying something most folks didn't realize they were selling."

Ethel pinched her lips tight and shook her head. Tears rolled down her cheeks.

"Suzanne told me that you walked in on Simon and her. How many other girls did you walk in on while Simon—" I couldn't bring myself to finish the sentence. Tears ran down my own cheeks. "It's not a secret you can keep anymore."

Ethel still didn't say anything, but her shoulders slumped. She covered her face in her hand. "They were tramps. All of them. The way they sashayed around him. It was shameful. Just shameful." She slid her hand to her throat. Her words sounded practiced but not convincing.

"Stop blaming the girls."

"Look at them all now if you don't believe me. Hardly a one is a good Christian girl with a family." Her tears had slowed. She'd moved to the offense.

"I couldn't agree with you more. They're still running in their own ways from what Simon did to them."

"*If* he truly did what you're saying, then they need to forgive him and get on with their lives."

"Don't you think 'I'm sorry' should come first?"

"He's dead. He can't say it."

"But you can."

"I didn't do anything wrong."

"You let it happen, Ethel. You looked the other way, and you never tried to stop it." I chewed on my lip a moment, afraid and nervous. "Even when it was happening to your own daughters."

She let a sob slip through, then caught herself.

"Those girls do need to forgive Simon and forgive you. But what are they forgiving if there's been no change in you? How can it be from the heart? How can those words be anything but empty?"

I stood up to go. I'd said all I could say. Now she had to decide for herself. "I brought you one more thing, Ethel." I pulled two sheets of folded paper out of my pocket. "Here is the list of girls and their addresses. It's from the trial, so some of the addresses might be wrong. You might know of some girls we missed."

She stared at the paper but wouldn't touch it.

"It's not too late, even for the saddest of the lot out there. You tell them you're sorry—tell it from your heart so that it's real. Then maybe they'll be able to forgive Simon and you."

Maybe they'd even be able to forgive themselves.

CHAPTER 24

THAT CHRISTMAS, THE ENTIRE COUNTRY was weary of strangers in green uniforms delivering telegrams, of empty stores and cupboards, of tissue-thin letters from folks we hardly knew anymore, of a world that was no longer black and white. We sang along with Bing Crosby *I'll be home for Christmas,* but for over four hundred thousand mothers, the song had a cruel edge to it. Mr. Crosby didn't mean it that way, I'm sure.

Those weeks I was home for Christmas, Mama's mood draped everything in a gray shroud. Mealtimes, choring, church trips, and Dad and me. Even the sky and wind stayed the color of steel. The clouds hung low, sometimes spritzing a little icy rain or small snow pellets but never letting loose a single shaft of yellow light. Oddly, what struck me most about those days, though, wasn't the heaviness of Mama's days and nights, but that Dad could survive the gloomy months with her and not get dragged down into her bottomless despair.

I know Dad hoped that my being home would lift her heart a little. But sometimes, what you have left only reminds you of what you lost.

Every day, I managed to get Mama out of bed and dressed. I made her come to the table to eat even though she mostly just pushed the food on her plate from one side to the other. I made her sit at the table with me while I wrote Christmas letters and worked a jigsaw puzzle. I think she'd just plain forgotten how to smile. Dad and I coaxed her to go to church on Sunday mornings and evenings and Christmas Eve. But that might not have been as much our doing as much as it was the powerful drive to keep up a pretense of normalcy in front of the church family.

Sadly enough, sometimes the very people who could best wrap you in their comforting arms and sustain you are the very ones you can't admit your frailty to.

Both Henry Schmidt and Ethel Yoder came to the Christmas Eve service. Ethel wouldn't look at me, but Henry lowered his invisible fence for a moment and shook my hand. He smiled a little, too. Marie had died two years ago that night and he hadn't had a child living at home since the funeral.

Maybe there was hope for Mama to smile again.

In between Christmas and New Year's, I put Mama in the car and the two of us took fresh cinnamon rolls to the Fitches and Henry. Henry made it easy for us. He let the screen door slam behind him and met the car as we pulled to a stop by the summer porch. I knew what his kitchen looked like. I'm sure he preferred not to have even more witnesses.

The wind flew into the car through Mama's open window as we talked a minute.

At Martha's, Mama just wanted to sit in the car and wait for me, but I wouldn't give in. It probably helped that the whole herd of Fitch boys came flying around the corner of the barn, two of them on a sheep, all of them with sticks.

"They wouldn't intentionally hurt a flea, Mama," I said, thinking to myself about how important a word like "intentionally" could be.

Her eyes widened.

"It'll get cold just sitting out here."

Mama sighed and climbed out of the car. She tucked her coat around herself against the knife-sharp wind and watched over her shoulder for wayward sheep, sticks, and boys as we blew to the house.

Sweetpea oozed her charm all over Mama, even though Mama'd brought her gray shroud along and was already draping it all over the Fitch world in spite of herself. Sweetpea either didn't care or instinctively felt called to convert Mama from her sadness. I guess even babies can have a mission.

Martha, Mama, and I visited at the kitchen table over Postum and sorghum cookies, although Martha and I did all the talking. Sweetpea hung on to Martha's apron, but she crept closer and closer to Mama and eventually laid her pudgy fingers on Mama's knee, so she had a hand in both worlds—her mama's yellow warmth and my mama's gray melancholy. Then she started puckering up and making smooching noises. She blew the invisible kisses at Mama whose face, it seemed with each kiss, gradually lost a tiny bit of its hollow, hard angles. Mama began breaking off small pieces of her cookie and feeding Sweetpea, who joyfully opened her mouth like a baby bird for worms. Her feet started dancing, one chubby leg lifted straight up then the other in no particular rhythm. Before long, Mama bent over and kissed Sweetpea's forehead. She smiled, too, the first I'd seen since I'd come home for vacation.

Martha and I could hardly carry on our conversation. This momentary transformation was electric and we both saw it.

"You could borrow her for a couple afternoons a week, Rose," Martha said and laughed. "The boys, too, but I'd have to send some rope along so you could tie them to a chair when they got out of hand."

Mama smiled softly. "This little girl just warms up a heart, doesn't she?"

"She does indeedy," Martha said. "The boys do, too, but in an entirely different way."

Mama nodded her head. "You're lucky you have so many."

"Most days I think that, too."

"This wound in my heart will never heal over." It sounded like a non sequitur, but it wasn't.

"We pray for you every day."

Mama's eyes grew wet. That was good. She'd had so little emotion these weeks.

"Thank you. I can't do it myself anymore."

"What? Pray?" Martha was surprised. I wasn't.

"How can I pray anymore?"

"You can't give up hope. He could come home."

"It's not about hope or faith or any of those. Even if he's alive, what cross will he have to bear forever? And if he's not, what cross will Ezra and I—" she abandoned the rest of the thought.

"The good Lord never gives you more than you can bear."

"Martha, do you really believe that?"

Sweet, kind Martha paused a long time. Then she finally said, "No."

"Neither do I. I never did before this and now I surely don't. The good Lord gives us more than we can bear all the time."

"Then what do we do?"

"We pray. That's how we keep going. But I can't pray anymore. I can't get out of bed most days. I can't get dressed or eat or even stand in my garden. But the most awful thing is that I just can't even say the words 'dear God.' I don't know how I'll keep going."

The lump in my throat matched the lump in my stomach.

"Mama, don't talk like that."

"It's true, Cat. You're an adult now. You should deal with truth instead of what everyone else wants you to believe. In the long run, there's less pain."

Another flamingo insight.

Martha and I were friends—good friends, but Mama and Martha were only neighbors, so everything Mama said that afternoon fell more into the confession category than the usual idle talk over a cup of Postum. Martha seemed to draw that kind of talk out of people in the same way that Mama used to in the days before Ben left us.

"We should go," Mama said even though she had nothing to do at home. She leaned down and kissed Sweatpea one more time. The baby girl finally released her mama's apron and reached up to Mama with both arms. Mama lifted her and took one last smooch from her, then set her down.

The two of us leaned into the biting wind and climbed into the car. The farmyard was empty of male Fitches, but I still carefully started the car and made a slow loop back toward the road. You never knew when one of those boys would decide that was the day to study the undercarriage of a car. I wanted to give them plenty of time to drop off before I picked up speed.

As we passed the house again, Martha came running out towards the car. She'd thrown one of LeRoy's choring jackets over her shoulders but hadn't bothered to stick her arms through the sleeves.

Mama rolled down her window just as Martha reached the car.

"Here." She pressed a string of colored beads into Mama's hand. "It's a rosary. It's a long story, but it belonged to my Great-Aunt Minnie who grew up a good Baptist like the rest of us. She married a Catholic boy and the family stopped talking to her for doing such a heathen thing. I would still sneak over to see her 'cause she was kind and funny. She left me her rosary when she died. She told me once she'd said ten thousand prayers on every bead." Martha closed Mama's fingers over the beads. "Just hold it, Rose. Hold it until you can find the words again. Carry someone else's prayers with you until you can pray your own."

Dad would have done any number of things, but Mama just nodded her head and whispered, "Amen."

CHAPTER 25

ALMOST FIVE HUNDRED YEARS EARLIER, Mennonites had nearly thrown the baby out with the bathwater. When we painfully extracted ourselves from the Catholic Church, we left behind pageantry, liturgy, confessionals, and popes. We also left behind most of what a body could see, hear, smell, touch, and taste: statues and rose windows, echoes and bells in cavernous spaces, incense and candles, rosaries and holy water, the body and the blood. We kept communion a couple times a year and added foot washing. But we stayed cerebral. We were a theology of the head and then of the heart, with the body a distant and unimportant last.

Mama had worn her gauzy white prayer covering part of every day since the day she'd been baptized in a muddy Kansas creek. It, too, carried her prayers, tens of thousands of them. But its familiarity dulled its meaning and it might as well have been the hankie she stashed in her pocket. This magical string of beads she could stroke and count. She knew what it meant to pray unnumbered prayers, and now she not only carried her own prayers in her own covering, she carried someone else's.

The weight of those Catholic prayers in her apron pocket made a visible difference. Before I left for school again, Mama started getting up on her own and combing her hair. Dad didn't know it, but even his shoulders drooped a little less because of that Baptist-turned-papist lady and her pagan beads.

I returned to the womb of college, glad to be concentrating on Yeats and T.S. Eliot instead of the deep well of problems of Suzanne, Henry, and Mama. The war didn't leave, though it crept closer to an end. Sam still wrote almost weekly. Even then, the longer we were apart, the more foreign his sentences became, the occasional reference to James & James notwithstanding. There was still a sweetness to his letters, but I hardly knew him anymore. Before the war, we'd had a trial and a host of Latin phrases in common. Now we had years of loneliness and loss. It might have been enough on which to learn to love each other, but then we could probably learn to love thousands of others, since that was something everyone shared. Robert Miller still wrote occasionally. His letters were filled with the familiar, but ironically, I wasn't drawn to Robert's familiarity as much as Sam's sweetness. They both wrote about the changing world, but from opposite ends of it.

College insulated my classmates and me from the real world and even the war. We got news like everyone else, but in retrospect, we took in slivers of the whole. To a certain extent, maybe we'd even lost our ability to absorb more than the slivers.

I was struck that January about how enveloped we were in a cocoon. When the Allies came across the gates of Auschwitz, I'm sure it was in all the newspapers and on the radio. But the horrors of what the Nazi machine had been doing didn't register until several weeks later when I'd dashed into the library in between classes to find a biography of Madame Curie for a paper I was working on. I heard Pearl's voice—you could never *not* hear my roommate's voice—a stack away. She and Ruth Yutzy were looking at some magazine and doing a lot of intense whispering.

Pearl's words were the clearest. "How awful! How horrible!"

Ruth kept her voice softer, so I couldn't understand the words, but I heard lots of small gasps and distressed *Oh!s.*

I was in such a hurry, I probably wouldn't have even remembered later except that then Pearl said, "Oh, my goodness! Don't ever let Cat see this. It would tear her apart."

I stopped looking at Dewey decimal numbers and peered through the gaps between books. They were looking at some magazine, I could see that much, but I couldn't tell what it was. I wanted to say, *See what?* but I was frozen to my spot. For all I knew, they could have been looking at a picture of Ben in the shadows of a Nazi and a noose.

Ruth said something else, and then Pearl said, "If they do this to just regular people, what would they do to their prisoners of war?"

I felt tingly.

It was that same feeling I'd had the days and weeks after we got the telegram. I didn't know if my feet would move, but I couldn't hear even Pearl anymore because my heart pounded loudly in my ears. Gertie Drescher, the librarian, joined Pearl and Ruth for a minute. She must have told them to be quiet because Pearl put the magazine back on the rack and then the three of them left. I stayed stuck to the linoleum as I tried to get my body to follow my brain. They stayed disconnected, but somehow I found myself in front of the magazines.

Auschwitz. It murmured from nearly every cover. I opened up *Life* magazine. It would show me the truth, only I wasn't ready for it. Skin-covered skeletons and big, empty doe eyes stared back at me. I sat down because I was pretty sure my legs weren't working anymore. It was a picture of stripes: horizontal lines of barbed wire, vertical stripes on their pajama-like garb. Vertical stick-bodies.

I stared at the pictures but I couldn't understand what I saw since the shapes looked human—human but devoid of spirit or life. It was as though something powerful had sucked out everything physical, emotional, and spiritual, leaving only skin that stretched across bones. The stick bodies were almost a child's drawing. They looked the same, each of them—only a nose or chin variation. Did they feel the same on the inside? Were they all walking cadavers or did they still have that essence that is the spark of difference for each of us?

I could only pick out words of the captions through my tears: *zombie, atrocity, crematorium, cattle-like.*

Hellhole. It was a word you never saw in print. It carried the weight of a thousand other words that could be printed.

Was this what we were fighting? How could people do this to people? Pearl was right. What would they do to an enemy? I didn't want Mama to be right, that Ben was better off dead. But looking at those pictures, I knew she was a flamingo once again. Unexplainably, I was mad at Mama, that she'd known all along and that Dad and I were silly Pollyannas. Unexplainably, too, I was mad at being a Mennonite. It was wrong. Every bit of it. The Nazis, the war, the bombings. Killing them could have solved something I told myself, even while I knew that killing would only feel good. It couldn't carve the deep depravity out of human hearts that let people do that to their own kind.

I finally left the library and went back to lie down in my room. I stared at the ceiling; the swirled plaster pattern swam in circles above me. Not a prayer covering or even a rosary would help me. I prayed Mama would never see those pictures.

CHAPTER 26

Sugar and spice
and everything nice
That's what our
Catherine Marie
is made of.
Born: February 4, 1945
Weight: 6 lbs, 10 ozs
Length: 21 ½ inches
Proud Parents: Charlie and Mona Beeb Dunbar

THE ANNOUNCEMENT ARRIVED IN A baby-pink envelope the end of February. Maybe the Baumgartner sisters—Martha and Mona Beeb—thought little girls were made of sugar and spice, especially since the little Fitch boys were certainly made of snakes and snails and puppy-dog tails. Still, when I sent my crocheted baby blanket, I wanted to add a P.S. to my congratulations letter: *Brace yourselves.*

But I didn't. That baby's mother had been many wonderful things at one time or another, but she wasn't ever sugar and spice. I suspected Charlie and Mona Beeb already knew they had something closer in kin to one of those Mexican chili peppers, but you can't put that in a baby announcement.

To my question about Suzanne's new address, Mona Beeb only wrote that Suzanne had returned to her sister's place in Wichita in late February. She hoped to get on again at Boeing but was worried that with the war winding down, they were already starting to lay people off and probably wouldn't take her back. Mona Beeb had no editorial comments.

I sent a letter to Suzanne at Anna Joy's. It was a cautious one. I thanked her for naming the baby after me. I told her my *grossmutter* and Catherine the Great appreciated it, too, although since they were both dead, I hoped she wasn't trying to impress them or anything. What I really wanted to know but couldn't ask was this: Now what are you going to do?

Suzanne didn't write back. Instead, she and her cardboard suitcase arrived in my dorm room on a rainy Wednesday afternoon in March.

"I suppose you think I'm going to mop the floor after you," Pearl said when Suzanne walked in dripping like a drowned rat.

"All the way down the hall and front steps if you don't mind." Suzanne flashed her best friend-winning smile.

Pearl rolled her eyes but laughed and went after the floor mop.

"Can I stay?"

"Sure." I tried not to stare at the suitcase.

"Just for a night or two. I promise."

"Sure." I hope I didn't sound too relieved. "I got the baby announcement. Did you get my letter?"

She nodded. "She's a beautiful baby." Her voice cracked.

"It was nice of you to name her after me."

"Better after you than after me." She smiled again, but it looked more like she was trying not to cry.

I chewed my lip a little. "You didn't get on at Boeing again?"

She shook her head.

I wanted to ask what she was going to do, but the suitcase and surprise visit already told me the answer.

"How's Anna Joy doing?"

"Same." She took in a sharp breath. "Burl's the same, too."

The baby, no job, bad brother-in-law. I had to stop asking questions. I think I was drumming my fingers on my desk.

Pearl came back with the mop.

Suzanne took it and started swiping the floor back in the direction of her tracks.

"She doesn't look too good," Pearl whispered.

I shook my head. "She's not."

Pearl knew me well enough to know she wasn't going to get any more out of me and went back to studying.

By the time we went to dinner, the rain had stopped. It left mud everywhere and crisp, damp air, but no wind. In its own way, it was a beautiful evening. Suzanne charmed the table in her usual way with endless stories about her good friends she'd spent some time with in Wynona, Oklahoma. There was no mention of why she'd spent that much time there, but no one seemed to notice, probably not even Pearl. And these folks now had two years of a college education.

Afterward, the two of us walked downtown so we could at least be on sidewalks and not in the mud.

"I want a cigarette," Suzanne said, almost within earshot of the college arches.

"You can't."

She rolled her eyes.

"You're a girl. This is a small town. I still have two more months of school."

"They wouldn't let you graduate if I smoke a cigarette?"

I gave her a half smile, but she didn't dig out her cigarettes.

We ended up on a bench in front of the post office. It was after six, so the town was shut down, even Emil's Cafe, which closed at two Monday through Thursday.

"Hear anything about Ben?"

I shook my head. "It's killing Mama." How long could a string of rosary beads last? "She can't bear the pain of not knowing. If he's dead, she won't be able to bear that either."

She nodded. "Dess. You don't know how that took the family down."

I thought I did, but we all assumed a lot about a lot of things those years. Most of them weren't right.

"Mom disappeared into her room. There was nothing. She never put dinner on the table. She could hardly put a comb through her hair."

I felt dizzy thinking about Mama.

But Suzanne wasn't done. "She couldn't even save herself, let alone us."

I took a deep breath to hold back the tears—for me, for her, for all of us.

We sat without saying anything for a long time. A single car drove past and the driver waved. It was good it wasn't the town policeman, or he would have felt obligated to stop and quiz us. I think he quit at five, though, so we were safe unless someone called him, nervous about two girls sitting in front of the post office when the whole downtown was closed.

Finally, Suzanne pulled a lavender envelope out of her pocket. "Did you get one of these?"

My stomach churned. My own lavender envelope had arrived late last week.

"From Ethel Yoder?"

"The one and only." There was a rueful tone in her voice. She took out the single sheet of paper and handed it to me.

I already knew what it said, but I read it anyway.

Dear Suzanne,
I am sorry for what Simon did to you. I am sorry I didn't do more to stop him.
Sincerely,
Ethel Yoder

The paper shook as I read it. I guess I never thought she'd write those words to each of us. "Did Anna Joy get one, too?"

Suzanne nodded. "She tore it up into little pieces and then burned it. She said it was about fifteen years too late."

"Is it?" I wanted to know what Suzanne thought. I handed the paper back to her.

It shook in her hands, too. "I don't know." She chewed on her lip. "How can it ever be wrong to say, 'I'm sorry'?"

"I don't think it can be unless she didn't mean it."

"Do you think she would have sent it if she didn't mean it?"

I thought about this a long time before I answered. In fact, I'd had three months to do my thinking. "Never."

"You know," she said and then paused so long I wasn't sure if she would finish the thought, "that's not the one I need to hear it from."

"He's dead."

"Not yet. But it's not because I haven't thought about it."

I didn't sleep well that night or any of the nights until Suzanne left the following Saturday, bound for as far as the bus would take her on eight dollars. That gave us too much time to walk every night into the evening light and talk about what she really would be doing next. All the unhappy stories, the cigarette smoke, the caustic commentary left us both with fitful dreams. Suzanne wasn't healing as much as she was scarring over, and it was deep and ugly. Underneath it all, through every vein in her body, she carried a river of sad and bitter waters that I'm not sure even Mama would understand.

"I just ache inside all the time," Suzanne said more than once as we walked. It was a cold week, even with spring near. Every night the wind bit through our thin wool coats and made us wish the war would finally, once and for all end, if for no reason than we couldn't take another winter of shivering for four months out of the year every time we stepped outside. One night she kept talking. "I thought after I had the—" she stopped and sighed a couple of times. "I thought when I left Charlie and Mona Beeb's that it would get better. But it didn't."

"It probably doesn't matter how you lose a child. It's your flesh and blood." Mama could have said it better.

"It's not just that. It's Simon. It's all of it. He destroyed me."

I fiddled with the hole that had worked its way into my coat pocket and kept my mouth shut. There were two parts to her story. The second part seemed to have been forgotten.

When Suzanne finally headed off to Denver, or wherever that money would take her, I believed it could be the last time I'd ever see her.

CHAPTER 27

In April, the world shifted yet one more time on its axis. The good died, the bad was shot, and the evil committed suicide.

On April twelfth, Franklin Delano Roosevelt crossed over to the glory land, if that's where Episcopalians go. He'd been, for all practical purposes, the only president I'd known. He'd led us out of the Great Depression and into war, but he also was leading us out of war. There was hardly an American who didn't honor the man and all he stood for.

Across the ocean, Mussolini, who'd apparently tired of his cushy puppet state the Germans had set him up in, set off for Switzerland with his mistress, a few followers, and a fortune in gold. On April twenty-eight, Italians, who had lots of reasons to be angry with what Mussolini had led them into, caught him and shot him.

And finally, on April thirtieth, the man who'd started the world's misery took the coward's way out. Adolph Hitler married his mistress, Eva Braun, then shot himself.

Within days, Germany surrendered and the war was over in Europe. The country celebrated something fierce. Even the college, as Mennonite as it was, stuck little toothpick flags in pieces of sorghum cake, a weird sight amidst all the prayer coverings. It was the week before finals and it made us all giddy to have that part of the war over.

Now, the worst part of waiting began. I wrote a letter to Dad and Mama telling them that the first they heard anything—anything about Ben, they were supposed to call the college or send me a telegram. After that much waiting, what was the profit from a few bushels of wheat?

Dad wrote a short note back. The wheat was doing good. They'd heard nothing from the government about Ben. Mama had taken to staying in bed most of the day again.

After the reprieve this spring, I could hardly bear the thought of Mama's return to that hollow shell. Even getting a note from Sam saying he'd be home for good this summer couldn't lift me out of my own restless sadness. The hopeful asides to James & James the past couple of years should have given me something to look forward to, but like everything else it felt hollow. More like a talisman than a promise.

Dad managed to put Mama in the car and bring her to my graduation. They got up before dawn on Sunday and drove victory speed the whole hundred and twenty miles to Hesston so they could be there in time for the baccalaureate service on Sunday morning. Even though I was only getting an Associate of Arts degree, it was still more education than anyone in our family had ever seen except for Mama's mother, who'd taught college Latin. I'd probably had more schooling than my dad's whole family tree put together. I could have gotten a big head, especially since it seemed half the church drove over for graduation in the afternoon. It didn't matter that at least half of those folks had relatives in Harvey County and saw my graduation as a good excuse to drive on over and spend some time with siblings and cousins they hadn't seen since the beginning of the war.

Even Henry Schmidt came. He gave me two crisp dollar bills.

Dad and Mama arrived only a few minutes before the church service started. I saw them slip into the pew, Dad in his Sunday suit, carrying his Sunday fedora. Mama wore the same pink dress and beet-dyed matching pink gloves she'd worn to my eighth grade graduation and my high school graduation. The dress drooped all over her body now, though, so even though she truly looked a bit like the flamingo she was, it was an aging flamingo.

All across America that month, graduation sermons and speeches rang with patriotic, God-loves-America talk. We'd won the war in Europe, and we were near victory in Asia. Surely, God was on our side. As Mennonites, we'd stayed clear of all the patriotic talk during the war and weren't about to follow that path now, so our baccalaureate and commencement services were more of a hymn to the goodness in the world. During the baccalaureate, we sang richly textured songs by German composers and heard vignettes from folks who'd spent time on the mission fields around the world: Japan, China, Argentina, Brazil, and Nigeria. No doubt, God loved Americans, but he also loved his other children around the world, who in recent years had suffered mightily.

We hadn't lost our houses and fields to bombs. Nor had we lost entire families to the ugly terror of a concentration camp. Still, a couple of the speakers seemed to pause a moment. Maybe they saw the lady in the pink dress and beet-dyed matching pink gloves stiffen.

A loss is a loss. If it's yours, it's never a relative thing.

D.H. Bender gave the commencement address. Peter Kaufman, who'd served the entire war in Civilian Public Service in the Ohio state mental hospital, shared stories of bringing wholeness to people who had only lived with cruel institutional neglect. He talked about going on to college and becoming a psychiatrist. He wasn't done changing the world.

It was a good Mennonite sendoff: "Go and do." In this case, the go and do involved a lot more education, which was politely ignored by most of the folks sitting on those hard wooden seats. Forty-two out of forty-five of my fellow graduates were women. Even Gladys Bontrager, valedictorian and science prodigy, hadn't broached the subject of another two years of college with her dad. She said he was already distressed enough that she had too much education to be a good farmer's wife.

When I'd talked to Dad about my own plans to finish college, we'd both had fidgeted. We came to a somewhat unhappy truce: I would get a teaching job for the coming school year and save that money for college for the following year. It meant we could both live with hope for the coming year that things would change. His hope would be that I'd give up this college foolishness. My hope would be that he'd finally let me make my own decisions.

At least he didn't say, "Absolutely not." But I'd guess he already figured out that was the wrong answer.

We should have had a pattern to our summers by now. Ben hadn't been home for years, and for the last two summers we hadn't known if he would ever be home again. LeRoy and Martha Fitch begged me to come back for the summer—Martha was starting to plump up with her next Fitch rabbit—so I should have just started up where I'd left off the August before, saddling up Little Willy and riding my way across the fields.

But somehow, victory in Europe had left the three of us at loose ends. Until we knew about Ben, there was no such thing as going on with life. We just couldn't. Dad tinkered with equipment in the barn, getting ready for harvest. And Mama would have stayed in bed all day, every day, never eating, never smiling, no longer even talking. I made her get up every morning, though, and sit outside in a green metal yard chair under the elm tree by the garden and close to the lilac bushes that were wildly fragrant that year. It was as if they knew that Mama's final hope rested on them. She still carried Martha's aunt's rosary in her apron pocket, but she told me she'd already used up those prayers and now just wanted to go home.

"You *are* home, Mama."

She looked at me and barely shook her head.

I didn't want to understand, so I fussed with cleaning out the flowerbeds around the house. That had never been my job. Mine had always been to mop the kitchen floor or run the wash through the wringer while Mama made her world fresh again.

But that became our pattern. If we'd thought about it, we'd have realized we were just waiting.

Toward the end of the first week, I sat with Mama and wrote a letter to the US Army, asking them if they could just tell us what happened to Ben. Did they find him alive? Did they find evidence of his death? Did they hear from someone who might know what happened to him?

We knew they'd be too busy to answer, what with the war still in its vicious last throes in the Orient, but it seemed like such a small thing to ask from them, given that we'd offered the ultimate sacrifice of our own flesh and blood and done it knowing that it would come to no good and that all of it was wrong.

We prayed, too. We prayed, of course, at mealtimes and bedtimes, and because Mama couldn't pray anymore, I took to praying with her out in the garden during the day. I prayed for strength and courage, for the ability to forgive the Germans for whatever they did to Ben and the US Army for not telling us anything. For the bravery to accept whatever God had handed us. Lots of times when we prayed, I didn't talk, we only listened, often with our eyes open. Mama needed to see the roses and the morning glories.

Sometime just before harvest started, Mama and I were sitting and listening in the garden one morning. A mile or so away, a car flew toward us, its giant brown dust plume announcing its arrival long before we could see the sleek black body.

Mama stood up. "Ben's home," she said simply.

I laughed. "Mama. You're talking like Gramma used to."

"It's true. Ben's home." She started walking toward the barn and the giant cottonwood.

Dad stepped out of the barn and pushed his hat back. He'd heard the car too. Maybe he'd heard God as well.

"Looks like Hank Burnum." He lifted his hat and scratched his head.

"From the elevator? Where's he going out this way?"

Instead of shooting past our lane, the car slowed and turned in.

"He's bringing Ben home."

"Mama!"

Hank rolled to a stop under the cottonwood. The pillow of dust settled slowly behind his car, coating everything green in fine silt. Hank had a passenger who got out of the car and just stood. Army green hung on his gaunt body. His eyes were giant eyes in a thin, pale face. Dad and I thought this was some army boy Hank Burnum knew, or someone who might have even known Ben and had come to tell us some truth.

Only Mama recognized him.

She whispered his name. "Ben."

"Mama, it's not Ben." Would she be like this forever? Calling every army boy Ben?

And then she ran towards him, calling him over and over.

Then the scarecrow of a man lifted his arms up and began running and reaching towards us. "Mama! Dad! Cat!"

I could hear him laugh.

"I'm home!"

$$\text{\textbf{—— CHAPTER 28 ——}}$$

We killed the fatted calf and held a feast for the prodigal son. Well, actually, Dad butchered a plump young chicken, which a miraculously revived Mama fried up while I worked on Ben's favorite dessert. And he didn't feel prodigal to us anymore because he was finally home. None of us cared about the path that had taken him away in the first place, except to be sorry we hadn't tried harder to divert it.

That's how it always is, isn't it? Whenever you're in the middle of a fight, it seems the only way out is to continue the direction you've fallen into. It's only in looking back that you see how pointless it was to dig your heels in or deliver the next blow.

The war had wounded us all in too many ways. Dad would carry his guilt and Mama the scars of her sadness. I would always carry the burden of not having done enough somehow, although I'm not sure what I could have done differently. But it's not such an uncommon badge to wear under the circumstances.

And then there was Ben.

We didn't recognize the shell of this man sitting at our dinner table. Even his body shape had changed. He was taller, maybe broader, but mostly bones. His skin stretched tight across his frame. He looked, for all the world, like those concentration camp pictures in the magazines. The thing I'd been so horrified by—and it had been true.

We hardly recognized the essence of the person, either. Except for that initial outburst when he touched Peters' soil, we could hardly see the old Ben, the one who had a sly wit and a sure way. The basketball hero, the boy all the girls flirted with. The belligerent son. They were all gone. We couldn't tell yet who had taken that boy's place, except to know that he seemed empty.

"Have another piece of chicken," Mama urged. Ben had already eaten at least half of this one while Dad, Mama, and I nibbled at the rest.

"I can't. That's more meat than I ate the whole time I was in the prison camp put together."

The three of us cringed at the word "prison," but Ben didn't seem to notice.

"I was one of the lucky ones, though. They captured seven of us. Only two of us survived."

Mama put her fist to her mouth, but I could see her eyes getting wet.

"Maybe we shouldn't talk about that yet," I said and tilted my head slightly at Mama. "Mama was so sad about you. We thought we were going to lose her, too."

Ben nodded slowly, but he looked a little confused. "We have to talk about it sometime. It can't just stay inside all of us. You have to know."

I nodded too. "Just not today. Today let's just celebrate that you're here in one piece."

Ben lifted a corner of his mouth. It wasn't quite a smile, but there was a little emotion behind it. He nodded again. "Sure."

I scooted my chair back and collected the dishes off the table while Mama cut the apple pie I'd made. She put a piece in front of Ben. "Cat made your favorite dessert. You probably didn't have any of this in . . . over there, either."

We all watched him, expecting some kind of excitement or happy reaction or something. Instead, he pushed the pie to the center of the table and rested his head on his open palms. He breathed deeply and slowly.

"If you're too full—"

He shook his head. He rubbed his face with his hands. "It's not that."

We waited. We weren't sure what for.

Finally, he spread his hands on the table and looked at the pie, but not with anticipation. It was as though he couldn't—or wouldn't—touch it. Then he slowly reached for it and pulled the plate back to him again. He turned the point of the pie toward himself, then away and picked up a fork. Each move was slow and deliberate, but there was no reverence to his movements. You'd have thought he was circling an enemy. He rested the fork on a fluted crust corner but didn't cut through the piece. Then once more, he turned the pie until the point faced him.

But instead of cutting it, he twisted his fork in his hand, around and around. He looked, well, wary. Finally, the fork came down, almost viciously, and he stabbed the point off of the pie and brought it to his mouth. The fork quivered. I'd been so intent on watching this strange dance between his hands, the pie, and the fork that I hadn't noticed his wet cheeks. My brother Ben was crying.

The pie on the fork hovered close to his mouth, and he looked at us. "This was my betrayal. Apple pie."

He took the bite and chewed slowly.

We waited and watched.

He swallowed and set his fork down. He wiped his eyes and cheeks, but those bones that only had skin stretched across still shook with emotion.

"That's what they did to trap us."

He stared at the pie.

"They brought out pieces of apple pie and set them down in front of each of us." He looked up at us. "Do you know how automatic it is that you turn the point of the pie towards you?"

We all looked at our pie pieces. The points stared back at each of us.

"It's automatic for those of us who grew up on pie. If you've never seen a piece of pie, you'll start at whatever corner the pie is put in front of you. Which, in this case, just always happened to be the crust corner." He took a deep breath. "Those of us Americans who would have preferred to stay, shall we say, unnoticed—" he paused carefully at the word, "reflexively turned our pies' points toward us and started eating. That's what gave us away."

He stopped talking and cut another bite, but he didn't eat it. "I told myself every day of those twenty-eight months that when—not if, but when—I got home again, I wasn't going to let the Germans take apple pie away from me. I was going to eat it and be glad for it." He finally put the pie in his mouth and chewed slowly. He closed his eyes and might have been praying, but I don't know that he could pray anymore.

After he swallowed, he opened his eyes again. "I'm not going to let them keep winning even after they've surrendered." He pressed his fork into the pie for another bite. "This apple pie is delicious, Cat." The words quivered with emotion, and I wasn't sure if he would really eat that bite.

Dad, Mama, and I still hadn't touched our pie. None of us wanted it anymore, ever, but Ben wouldn't let it alone. "You have to eat yours, too. You can't let the demon take control or there's lots more things you'll never do again."

Mama nodded. She knew in her own way.

"If it wasn't apple pie, it would have been something else." Ben smiled a little, but there weren't any crinkly lines around his eyes, so it wasn't a real smile. "It's true. There's a reason for everything."

CHAPTER 29

Dinner wore us out, but it was a giddy kind of wearing out. Dad and Mama wanted to put Ben in the car and drive him to every corner of the county to show him off. He'd made it home. He still had two legs, two arms, two eyes, and ten fingers, although some of those looked more crooked than we'd all remembered. He was as safe and sound in body as any of us could have hoped for.

Over the coming years, the stories that would explain what might be crooked on the inside would gradually ooze out of him like pus out of an infected wound—a story here, a story there, each one gradually more horrible than the last. He'd paint the canvas with the broad strokes of an incident. When we'd become sufficiently numb, he'd go back weeks or months or even years later and fill in a detail, a single slender stroke with a finer brush, letting us see into the dark places in his mind and soul just for a moment before he closed it off again.

Mama had been right about so many things. We would never fully have Ben back.

But that first day none of us—not even Ben—could comprehend how this would change our lives.

The meal wore out Mama and Ben. As soon as I finished the dishes, they both slipped away to their rooms—Mama to her cocoon that she'd wrapped herself in for 786 days, and Ben to the room that hadn't been his since he was an innocent boy. I wondered what he would think if he opened his trunk and saw how empty it was. We'd know, maybe, some day. But today he really did need to just sleep a little and fill his well. When they woke, we'd take off to see relatives and the church family. Dad promised we'd celebrate with supper at the Sweethome Café.

I saddled up a tired old Little Willy and took off through the pasture under a milk-white sky to tell the Fitches the wonderful news. The weather had been good that year: deep and soaking rains when we needed the moisture and dry hot days when we needed that. The wheat had never been more perfect. The ditches and pasture grass flowed a thick velvety green. The wheat stood waist high, drooping gently from the heavy, nearly bursting ripe heads. Sunflowers and black-eyed Susans waved from all corners of the pasture and fields. Even the crows looked fat and happy. They cawed to me, excited that the harvest would be rich this year.

I crested the last hill to the Schmidt farm. First the cottonwoods poked above the ground. Then the ridge of the barn's roof lined the horizon. Gradually the tattered barn grew larger and the house appeared, dusty gray and hopelessly shabby. Little Willy paused to nibble a little sweet grass. In all the trips to the Fitches', he'd never been able to shake the habit of stopping here, even if it was for only a moment.

Below me, the barn doors gaped open, as well as the haymow doors above it—a giant with an open mouth and a Cyclops eye. Summer hues swirled out of it and back in. Like a dream or a premonition, I couldn't tell. But for a moment, I expected Simon Yoder to fly backwards out of the eye in the barn.

Or Henry Schmidt.

Heat waves will do that. Colors appeared; mirages emerged. Another swirl of summer colors flew out of the haymow and back in. A wild halo of blond Schmidt curls floated above the colors.

Suzanne had come home.

The world stopped; I spurred Little Willy, but he wasn't ready to give up his tender green lunch. I dug my heels into his flanks again. He groaned and shifted forward slightly but refused to plod toward the barnyard. Finally, I slipped off Little Willy and flew down the slope. There could be no good reason for Suzanne to be home. There could be no good reason for Suzanne to be in the haymow.

"Suzanne? Suzanne?"

No voice responded.

"Henry?"

My heart thumped loudly in my ears, fogging my thinking.

"Suzanne?"

I stood in the center of the barnyard, not knowing if I should go into the house and ring the sheriff or head into the barn and up into the hayloft. The wrong choice would lose precious seconds.

Suzanne made my decision.

"What are *you* doing here?" She appeared in the haymow door, her hands on the beam above her, her feet barely touching the floor as she leaned out into the open air. The wind lifted and swirled her skirt.

"What are you doing here?"

"I'm waiting. Isn't that what prisoners do?"

"You're not a prisoner. You're free to make your own choices—"

"You think bars make a prisoner? You think only someone who goes two years without seeing a sunset is a prisoner? You don't know much about prison."

She lifted her feet and swung out. I held my breath and waited till she planted herself back on the floor.

"Where's your dad?"

"I don't *have* a dad."

"You have a father. He hasn't always been a good one, but you have one. Where is he?"

"If you mean Henry Schmidt, the man who sold his daughters one by one to the King of Kiowa County and then, for good measure, sold one of them a second time to the Kansas State prison system so she could spend the rest of her life wishing he were dead—I don't know where he is. But if you see him, you can tell him I'm waiting for him."

"Suzanne—"

"We have unfinished business." She swung out again. Dust scattered through the air behind her. The colors of her skirt lifted in the air. "I only did half the job before. I came to finish it."

To push or to jump? Maybe both. She left it unsaid.

"How will that make things better?"

"One of us will be out of our misery."

"And one will have greater misery."

"It's not possible. You live in a dream world, Cat."

"I'm coming up there."

"Why? You want to be part of the misery, too?" She laughed, but it was an empty, humorless noise. "Go home. You don't need to be a witness. For once, try to save yourself instead of trying to save me." She swung out again. "Don't you know by now it can't be done?"

I sighed. "Friends never learn things like that."

I hadn't been in that barn since a childhood so long ago that it might never have existed. Dad kept his barn clean enough for a potluck. Henry's was like I remembered it: full of rusting, wounded equipment and broken boards, piles of burlap bags and filthy feedsacks. Thick, silky tangles of spider webs stretched across nearly every surface. The dust clung to the air, giving me a fit of sneezes before I even reached the haymow ladder, the only spot—maybe on the whole farm—that had new boards nailed where the old ones had worn apart. Something fluttered against the rafters, sending another shower of dust down.

The haymow itself had a few stacks of moldy-smelling hay, but nothing fresh enough to feed a cow. I picked my way carefully across the thick scattering of ancient hay on the floor, finding the path that wouldn't give way under too quick a foot. Suzanne, her back turned to me, stood framed in the haymow door. Yellow afternoon light bathed the thick air around us, giving her an almost holy, otherworld cast.

But I wasn't confused. She hadn't come to do any good.

"Suzanne. I don't know what you're planning to do, but it's not a solution."

She turned around and I saw she was crying.

"Why do you think you always know what's right? You live this fairy-tale life and you think you know what I should do."

"Ben's home."

She paused, but only for a heartbeat. "See? Even your precious brother survives the war when millions around the world die. You lead a charmed life and you're too charmed to even know it."

"Suzanne." I took a slow breath. "You don't know—"

"Stop it! I don't want to hear it. I don't want to hear any of your easy answers. I'm the one who has to live in this pain—pain you can't fathom."

The putt, putt, putt of Henry's old pickup echoed to the west. Suzanne stretched her body in that direction, as though she'd be able to see over the hills.

"He's coming."

"Suzanne, you're not the only one in pain. Your dad is too."

"Good," she snapped. "In a few more minutes he'll be in more pain."

"How does making him hurt worse help you?" I wanted to grab her and shake her. She was a needle caught on a scratch in a record. She couldn't stop living in the middle of all of her hurts.

"Last summer and the summer before I rode past your place every morning on the way to the Fitches'. Every morning, Suzanne, your dad stood in the spot you're standing in now."

She wouldn't look at me, but her shoulders twitched.

"Every single morning."

"Good. He should have his own demons."

"Maybe you share the same demons."

I could see the truck's dust cloud rising up over the shimmering wheat fields and drifting eastward with the wind. He would turn into the lane in another minute or so. Below us, I heard Little Willy whinny softly in pleasure. He'd made it down the slope to the mulberry tree and found dessert.

"Maybe if you let some of your demons go, he'll be able to let go of his, too."

Suzanne glanced in Little Willy's direction, then watched the truck putter to the lane and turn in. She slumped to the floor, her back against the doorframe. One leg dangled outside against the splintery barn front. "He can let go first."

Henry stopped under a cottonwood. I heard the truck door slam, but I couldn't see him.

Immediately, he must have seen the riderless Little Willy. "Cat?" I could hear the joy in his voice. I tried to read Suzanne's face. Could she hear it? Did she know that sound in her father's voice?

"Cat?"

He came into view halfway between the barn and the house.

"She's here," Suzanne said. Her voice had a forced casualness to it, but you could still hear the tears. "And so am I."

He looked up at the Cyclops eye. "Suzanne?" His voice had greater joy. And something else.

She stood up and took hold of the beam above the door. She would swing again.

I grabbed a thick wad of her skirt. She would take us both down if she let go and I didn't.

She twisted around to me and hissed, "Stop it! Let go!"

"No." I said it loudly enough for Henry to hear, too. "She wants to finish her unfinished business, Henry. She wants to die."

"No! Suzanne, please! Don't!"

"It's too late."

She pulled back to swing out with more force, but I stood rock hard against the momentum.

"Let go of me," she growled.

"I won't." I wrapped the fabric tighter in my fist.

"No! No, it's not too late. Suzanne, I'm sorry. I'm more sorry than you'll ever know!"

"Stop it! It's too late to say you're sorry. Where were you when we tried to tell you about Simon? Tell me that!" She yanked on my wrist, trying to break free. I gripped onto her skirt with both hands now and tried to brace myself if she lunged. I had to hope she wouldn't want to take me with her.

"I know. I know. Every day I wonder how I could have been so stupid. How I could have worried so much about money that I lost you." He started to cry. He pulled his crumpled bandana out of his overalls pocket and mopped his face in big swiping motions. "I'm sorry. I'm so sorry." The words were jumbled up with tears, but you couldn't miss them.

"Don't. I don't want to hear it."

"You have to hear it. You have to know. I was wrong. I kept this rat-hole of a farm and lost everything. Everything. If you can't forgive me, I understand because I'll never, ever be able to forgive myself. But you have to hear me. I'm sorry! I'm so sorry!"

"Stop saying that. It's too late. You sent me to prison. You!"

"It was wrong. Terribly wrong. But I was so angry with you and how you humiliated me at Simon's funeral." He stopped and blew his nose. He took a deep breath. "I went crazy. I wanted to punish you, and so I told the sheriff what I knew. You pushed Simon. I saw it and I decided to tell." Deep, heaving sobs covered his next words.

"You destroyed me. Your own daughter." Her body was rigid and shaking.

"I know. And I destroyed myself when I did it." His whole body shuddered, full of anguish and tears. He pointed his finger up at Suzanne. "Every morning I stand at that spot. I wish I would have been the one to push or be pushed, not the one who's standing here now. I should have sacrificed my life for you."

"Why couldn't you have said all that years ago?"

"I say it every day, Suzanne. You're just not here to hear it. But now you are." He took another deep breath and pushed his tears away with the heel of his hand. "I love you. And I'm sorry I lost you in my own greed and blindness. I'm sorry."

Suzanne dropped her arms from the beam and covered her face. Tears gushed and her body shook with deep, cathartic sobs.

She turned and wrapped her arms tightly around me.

‹═══ CHAPTER 30 ═══›

I DON'T KNOW HOW ENTIRE countries forgive each other. It's not easy to say *I forgive you* when your child has been snatched from your arms and shipped like an animal off to be gassed and then cremated. I don't know how a person can look at piles of broken stones that once had been your home, your livelihood, your country—your hope and future—and say, *You were wrong, and I forgive you anyway.* To lose your loved ones, to lose all that defines you, to survive torture and the kind of pain that creates the deepest kind of shadows in your heart and mind—how do you say, *I will never be whole again because of this deep, dark hollow place you've created in my soul, and I forgive you anyway.*

I don't know how one person forgives another person. I don't know how someone can rob you of your childhood or innocence or of your own flesh and blood and say, *I know you did this. I can point to the time, place, and the choices you made to take the most precious thing I have away from me. You were wrong, and I forgive you anyway.*

I don't know.

I do know this, though: that without letting go, without some way of saying *that's in the past and this is now,* a body never can begin to fill in those deep etchings on the heart. And as long as those places are there, they'll catch whatever is bad or unhappy. They'll snare the rage and turn it into flames that, seemingly, can only be doused with greater rage.

I wish I could say that when Henry Schmidt told Suzanne he was sorry that she forgave him and their healing was sudden and complete, but that would make a sham of all the pain that had gone before that moment. It could no more be that way than if simply releasing Ben from that Nazi prisoner-of-war camp made him whole in body and spirit again.

It was a start, though. In those simple words, Henry unlocked Suzanne's prison doors. She had a chance to set herself free.

The first week of August, the United States Army sent us a letter saying that they had rescued Benjamin Dietrich Peters from a prisoner-of-war camp near Hammelburg, Germany. *Presently,* the letter told us, *your loved one is convalescing in a military hospital in London, England. Rest assured that he is safe and sound and is rapidly returning to full health.* They didn't think to mention the hole in his heart, but since it wasn't one that a plaster cast or a surgeon's stitches would ever mend, I guess they figured it didn't count. The United States Army seemed to have missed a lot, given that Ben was the one to walk out to the mailbox and open the letter.

That same week, we dropped an atomic bomb on Hiroshima, Japan. In case anyone in Japan was sleeping and missed the point of the first one, we dropped a second atomic bomb three days later on Nagasaki.

On August 14, 1945, the war ended. At least the bombs and the shooting part. Fifty-five million people died in World War II. Hundreds and hundreds of millions more suffered from wounds to their bodies or souls. It seems there should have been a better way to solve the problem of Hitler, but this was the only solution the world came up with. Unfortunately, we were sorely lacking in imagination those years.

Gradually, the world came home from war, or at least the part of the world that had a home to come to. Those who didn't gradually spread to parts of the Western hemisphere. They took with them some of the poison of the war, but they also brought the most enduring of human qualities: that tomorrow would be better. Hope survived.

Sometime in mid August, Kenny Kistle came home from his sojourn in hell. I ran into him in Wichita, of all places, when I was visiting Suzanne. I would never have recognized him, with his vacant eyes and skeleton frame, but he spotted me at the soda fountain at the Woolworth's store.

"Hey. Alley Cat. That you?"

I looked in the mirror behind the fountain boy and studied the reflections. As hollow as it sounded, I still knew the voice, but I couldn't tell which body it came out of.

"It's me." The third boy over from me lifted a forefinger, the Kansas wave. "Your old buddy Kenny."

"Kenny Kistle? You made it back!" A faint memory bubbled up that Mama had gotten this news from Mrs. Kistle. "You survived Bataan."

He slowly nodded his head. "Yup, and you were the gal I thought about every day."

My face felt hot. There were too many stupid things he could say in such a public place. The old Kenny would have sold his mother for such a sweet opportunity.

This Kenny slid off his stool and carried his cherry phosphate to the empty stool beside me. The sleeve of his right arm was flat and pinned to his shirt.

"Remember that dead rabbit we found on the way home from school that day? The day Kerm and I had all that rum?"

I nodded, trying to remember details. I could only remember he swung a fist—the fist he was missing now—at me, but I couldn't remember why. I tried not to stare at the flat sleeve.

"I told you to pray for me, that I wouldn't die. Remember that?"

"Vaguely." I remembered praying that he wouldn't die while he was off killing others. That part came back to me.

"Remember what you said after the prayer?"

I shook my head.

"You said, 'You have to be careful what you pray for because you just might get it.'" He shook his head and looked past me. There wasn't much on his face, but his eyes flickered. "You just might get it," he repeated and snorted softly. "I got it, Alley Cat. I got what I prayed for."

"But you're home safe now."

He nodded but didn't say anything for a while. Finally, he looked at me. "Well, at least the home part is right." He shrugged the shoulder of the missing arm. "Too bad I couldn't leave the memories the same place I left my arm."

We small-talked a few more minutes until Suzanne tugged me away. I'd already heard stories of dozens of Kenny Kistles, single drops in an ocean of pain. I didn't know if I had the courage to hear more.

Sam James returned that summer, too. We were strangers and intimate friends. Both of us had changed so much that it was hard to know where to start again. We'd been separated almost ten times as long as those five months we'd known each other, from the day we met till the day he kissed me and left. Still, I have to admit that when he drove up the lane in his mama's new car, my heart tripped all over itself.

I was glad Ben was home so the two of them could get reacquainted. It took a shade of the awkwardness away that first day. I watched them talk. At one point, they headed out to the pasture to bring in the cows. You could tell the two of them had their own secrets they shared, things they might never tell the rest of us about what they knew about the capacity of people to do evil.

Some secrets are better not known.

Soon after Sam came home, he drove me up to meet his mother, who lived in a solid red brick house on a quiet elm shaded street in Wichita.

He whistled "Lili Marleen" as we drove past fields of greening maize and ditches overflowing with black-eyed

Susans. He took my hand after we drove through Pratt and kissed it and said he'd missed me. He'd missed my humor and my innocence and my courage. None of which I even knew I possessed then or now.

When we drove through Hutchinson, he kissed my hand again and told me he was glad I hadn't fallen for some local boy during the war. That's what he'd worried about the most, even more than German bombs. And then we talked about how life could never be the same for any boy who'd gone off to war. I wanted to believe that it wouldn't be true for him, but he wouldn't let me live with that fairy tale. His eyes watered when he said it.

When we reached his mother's house, he squeezed my hand one last time. I hadn't expected him to be as nervous as I was.

Sam's mother was waiting for us on her crisp white front porch, along with a pitcher of fresh lemonade and homemade sugar cookies. The diminutive, well-kept woman had bright green eyes and a halo of coppery brown hair.

"Mother, I'd like you to meet Catherine Peters. Cat."

She smiled warmly and took my hand with both of her hands. "Sam has told me so much about you. I'm glad we finally get to meet under better circumstances."

"Cat, this is my mother, Alice Hibble."

"Hibble?"

"My dad died when I was young. Mother remarried Bernard Hibble when I was a teenager, but I kept my dad's name for a number of reasons."

"Hibble?" I said it again, trying to dredge up how I knew that name. "Did you used to live in Sweethome?"

She nodded. She had all the puzzle pieces and I was just now putting them together.

"Your husband was the banker who—" Polite company back then had no acceptable way to say "suicide."

She nodded again and looked at Sam who explained, "The family always blamed your dad and Simon Yoder that my stepdad took his own life."

I held my breath for what might be coming out of Sam's mouth next. Sam and his mother never would have known that my dad blamed himself for Bernard Hibble's death. They never would have realized he had his own sleepless nights, even though he was just trying to get Mr. Hibble to sign off on his loan papers—something the bankerman should have done a few hours earlier.

"I would still blame him today if I hadn't met your family. I know now that your dad just happened to be part of the last straw."

I breathed again, grateful this wouldn't forever be between us.

"I was there that night." I looked at Alice. "Do you remember the little girl? That was me."

Alice Hibble nodded. "I remember the little girl had some spunk to her. Think of the irony when Sam told me that this case brought those two people back into our lives, only they were on the opposite sides of a case."

"It didn't take long to realize which side I wanted to be on," Sam said. "Your father was and is a good man."

"Simon had always had his fingers in the bank," Alice said. "He was on the board, you know, and pushed Bernard to make a lot of loans that weren't good. Bernard saw what was happening but couldn't stand up to the pressure Simon put on him."

Sam smiled at me. "I had my own demons to fight in that trial. But I beat them and discovered you at the same time. Good can come out of bad."

Then he kissed me on the lips in front of the neighbors and his mother and God. I loved it.

And then he whispered in my ear, "James & James, Attorneys at Law? Will you say yes?"

I laughed, squeezed him tight, and kissed him again. "Yes! Yes, a thousand times yes!"

BOOK CLUB QUESTIONS

1. The original title for this trilogy was *The Secret War.* What are the important secrets that shaped the lives of the characters? At various times throughout the three books, Cat muses that some secrets are better not known. What are some of the secrets that would have been better not to know? Why? What are some of the secrets that seemed better not to know but turned out to be important ones to know?

2. In Chapter 9, Cat notes, "Patriotism is a religion." How is patriotism like a religion? How is it different? What is the impact when patriotism becomes a religion?

3. In his letter to the Peters family about Ben, Ernie Kowalski writes, "[Ben] confided in me that he made a conscious decision at some point to fight this evil, even if he lost part of his own soul doing it." In Chapter 13 Cat says, "[T]here weren't any more girls

after Suzanne. She was the final one. How many girls had she saved by sacrificing herself?" Both Ben and Susanne sacrificed themselves to stop evil. Yet only one is revered for this sacrifice. Why?

4. Forgiveness is an important theme in *Never Enough Lilacs*. In Chapter 23, Cat tells Ethel, "Those girls do need to forgive Simon and forgive you. But what are they forgiving if there's been no change in you? How can it be from the heart? How can those words be anything but empty?" Can there be forgiveness if there's been no change in the other person? Whom do you need to forgive? What will it take for you to forgive that person? Who needs to forgive you? What will it take that person to forgive you? What can happen if there is forgiveness?

5. In Chapter 30, Cat observes she doesn't know how entire countries forgive each other. Is it possible to forgive an entire country for their war aggressions? What happens if countries don't? What happens when countries do?

6. In the last chapter, Cat observes, "On August 14, 1945, the war ended. At least the bombs and the shooting part. Fifty-five million people died in World War II. Hundreds and hundreds of millions more suffered from wounds to their bodies or souls. It seems there should have been a better way to solve

the problem of Hitler, but this was the only solution the world came up with. Unfortunately, we were sorely lacking in imagination those years." It could be argued that the world is still lacking in imagination in how to resolve problems peacefully. What are specific things we could be doing as a country or as individuals to resolve problems more peacefully?

7. *Never Enough Flamingos* begins with this: "How you get to where you don't know you're going determines where you end up." Where will Cat, Suzanne, and Ben end up?

8. After having read the full trilogy, *Never Enough Flamingos, Never Enough Sisters,* and *Never Enough Lilacs,* what impact has the story had on you? Has your thinking shifted about anything? If so, in what way(s)? How has this impact changed your behaviors?

9. What will stay with you from the story?

ACKNOWLEDGMENTS

THIS TRILOGY HAS BEEN DECADES in the making, and I'm grateful that the last of the story is now complete. Much as my heart is wrapped up in Cat Peters' world, it's time for the characters to move on. Me too.

Since *Never Enough Flamingos* was first published in 2016, many readers have asked me if the story is autobiographical or the story of someone I know. To be clear, it's not my story or the story of any one person I know. Rather, it's the story of countless women I know—and that number increases as readers share their own experiences with me. Additionally, people ask if this is typical of Mennonites. The answer is no more and no less than any other social construct. Mennonites are the print on the fabric of the story. The warp and weave are about how anytime there's hierarchy and power, there are vulnerable people—always children, often women.

That said, I couldn't have written any of the trilogy without the countless stories I heard from my grandparents, parents, and in-laws about life in Kansas during the Depression and World War II. My father, who was a brave conscientious objector in World War II, riveted my sisters and me with his exotic stories of working in the Marlboro, New Jersey, State Mental Hospital during the war, which did work its way as a mention into this last book. Decades later I learned that only 3,000 conscientious objectors worked in mental hospitals during World War II, but they returned home determined to change the way mental illness is treated in the United States and were hugely successful at doing so. They impacted the world as surely as anyone who carried a gun in World War II.

As with *Never Enough Flamingos* and *Never Enough Sisters,* my mother-in-law, Doris Jantz Diller, who is my only surviving parent, will recognize details from her life that are woven into the work. Her details brought color to the story, but again, the story is not of her life or the life of any one single person I know. From Simon Yoder to Sam James, this is entirely a work of fiction.

I'm especially grateful for the help of those who read this manuscript in its many forms. Both my flamingo sister Patrice Dunbar and my flamingo friend Lisa Travis have never stopped supporting me and encouraging me. Without them, this trilogy would never have made it into the hands of readers. In addition, a huge thank you goes to the following people for their willingness to read, give feedback, and encourage me: Teresa Barnes, Dena Charlton, Sarah Conrad Yoder, Diana De Pry, Marjorie Ehrhardt, Nan Graber, Mardell Hochstetler, Kristi Lawrence, Marcia Mendez, and Gary Van Vorst.

I'm thankful, too, for Elizabeth Cameron, editor extraordinaire, who made the manuscript sing and gave me reason to believe this trilogy was worthy of publishing. My great appreciation also goes to Adam Turner, who took a design concept from Susan Bartel and turned it into a series of distinctive covers. I'm grateful for his eye, his speed, his design competence, and his patience.

And a final thanks to John Willems, who deserves special appreciation for all his real-life feedback on the historical accuracy, especially since the timing of this last book fell into the middle of a sad life transition, and yet he made time for this. I'm forever grateful.

My most important thanks goes to Steve, who has supported and encouraged my writing even when there didn't seem to be a reason. Thanks for being my flamingo—and my best friend.

ABOUT THE AUTHOR

JANELLE DILLER WAS BORN AND raised in Kansas. She'll forever have a soft spot in her heart for golden wheatfields, sunflower-filled ditches, and sunsets that explode colors on the horizon. Her Mennonite linage dates back to when the Anabaptist movement first grew out of the Swiss Reformation in the sixteenth century. Janelle is a true mongrel Mennonite, with Swiss, Dutch, German, and Russian Mennonite roots. She remains a member of the Mennonite church today and will forever love a cappella four-part harmony (with an occasional rousing piano accompaniment) and potlucks.

Currently, she and her husband divide their time between sailing the Mexican coast in the winter and spending summers in Colorado. In addition, she writes political thrillers for conspiracy lovers and early chapter book mysteries for the award winning Pack-n-Go Girls Adventure series. Someone forgot to tell her to stick with a single genre.

Janelle loves to connect with her readers in person when possible and on Skype with book clubs and classrooms. Contact her through her website at www.janellediller.com.